The Mystery
of the Missing Bracelets

Dorothy Martin

Moody Press
CHICAGO

1

Vickie stuffed her books onto the locker shelf, yanked out jacket and scarf, slammed the door shut, and elbowed her way through the crowded hall.

"Hey, Vickie. Want a ride? My mother's coming in about half an hour."

"No, thanks. I'm going to grab the 3:30 bus. I'm in a hurry to call Diane."

"How come she wasn't at school today?"

"She had a doctor's appointment. See you after Christmas."

Vickie dashed across the school yard, skidded on a patch of ice, and threw out her arms to catch her balance. She had better slow down. Catching the bus was not worth the risk of breaking a leg and spoiling the two weeks of Christmas vacation that stretched ahead.

The wait for the bus seemed longer today without Diane's zany comments to laugh at. Shivering in the wind that skimmed across the snowy street, Vickie thought back to the blistering July day when she and Diane had met and become instant friends.

Even now, five months later, she could still feel the loneliness of the weeks after they had moved into the city apartment in June. She had dreaded going to a new school with no friends. Having a famous lawyer father, an artist mother, and a sister who was a television reporter was no help when you had to make it on your own. Then she had met Diane, and their friendship had wiped out loneliness.

It was funny how well they clicked when they were such opposites. Diane was so positive about everything and had an opinion on every subject. She breezed through math and science and social studies as though they were second grade level instead of seventh. And she would be a whiz in sports if it were not for the body cast she had to wear because of the scoliosis that had twisted her spine.

"Just wait till next semester," Diane kept saying. "When this thing comes off, I'm going to be seventh grade volleyball champ."

Vickie doubled her fingers inside her mittens for warmth. Her lips curved in a smile at Diane's optimism. Diane knew she could not play volleyball or any other active sport for a year at least, but pretending helped.

And Diane insisted, "Vickie, you can do anything you want to, if you just try."

Maybe that was true for Diane, but when you have been average all your life, it was hard all of a sudden to change. The trouble was that all through grade school teachers had said, "Why, Vickie, you should be able to express yourself well when you have such a gifted father." Or, "Surely, Vickie, *you* can draw better than that. Your mother is so talented." And, worst of all, "Vickie, when Francine was in my class, she was always the leader." Somehow, she had been born just average into a talented family. And if that was the way you were, how could you change?

She spotted the bus coming a block away and, holding her red mitten in her teeth, fumbled in her shoulder bag for exact change. She climbed on, dropped in the fare, and plopped onto the vacant seat near the door.

"Where's your bouncy friend?"

4

The driver tossed the question over his shoulder as he checked the side mirror before swinging the bus out into the traffic.

"She had a doctor's appointment today."

"Oh, ho—getting an early start on vacation, eh?"

Vickie smiled back at his laugh and thought again how neat he was. The first time he had picked them up, he had watched Diane grab the railing on each side of the steps and slowly pull herself onto the bus. That first step up from the ground was hard for her to manage. After that, he always pulled the bus up close to the curb. He never rushed the little old lady who usually got on a couple of blocks from school, and he made sure she had a seat right by the door. He knew how to joke with the kids from school and still not let them be rowdy or blare transistors so that they bothered other passengers.

"Do you like driving a bus?" Diane asked him one day.

"Sure. Where else do you get to sit down on the job and pass the time of day with all the nice people who come along," he demanded in return, flashing them his cheerful grin.

Vickie did not often come up with the snappy answers to his remarks that Diane did. Today she smiled back at him and sat watching the blocks slip by until the bus reached her stop.

She stood up as he swooped to the curb. "I won't be taking this bus until after school starts. So, merry Christmas."

"Same to you. And have a good vacation. Don't forget—this is Tuesday, which means you've got only four days to finish your shopping. Say merry Christmas to your friend for me."

He lifted his hand in a wave as the doors closed. Vickie waited until the bus pulled away and then dashed across the street, the cold biting at her again.

Heavy clouds threatening snow, hung low over the tall buildings that Vickie could see looming against the downtown skyline. Even the top of their apartment building was shrouded in a spooky-looking mist. Vickie stopped on the corner and put her head back to look up the building. Their apartment was only on the eleventh floor, and she wondered what the sky looked like from the forty-second floor on a day like this.

"I'll ask Anna if she cleans any apartment up that high. Maybe she'll let me go up with her some day."

Her teeth chattering, Vickie hurried along the sidewalk to the carved white iron gates that separated the apartment complex from the street, then along the intersecting walks past the fountain that stood frozen in the center of the courtyard. She pushed through the revolving doors into the lobby and stopped by Mac's desk.

"Has my mother come home yet?"

He nodded and stepped over to unlock the inner lobby doors. "About an hour ago. She looked as frozen as you do."

"You'd better wear ear muffs when you go home," Vickie cautioned. "It's freezing out there."

Vickie pushed the button for the elevator and got on when the doors slid open silently. She pulled back her fur-lined hood and, yanking off the red knitted scarf, she fished the silver key chain from her bag. It was funny. When they had lived in their house, she had never thought about needing a key. Now, taking a key was as automatic as putting on her coat.

She unlocked the apartment door and sniffed hungrily. Mother was still baking Christmas cookies. The piny smell of the fat, long-needled wreath on the door mingled with the buttery smell of baking cookies to make

Christmas seem really close.

"Vickie?"

Mrs. Montgomery poked her head into the hall from the kitchen. "Your father is working late tonight on a case that comes to trial right after Christmas, so he won't be home for dinner. Francine is eating out with Pete. I thought you wouldn't mind our dinner being a little late so that I can finish these cookies. I'm almost ready to put the last batch in to bake, and then they will be ready to decorate. Want to help?"

"Sure."

Vickie stuffed her jacket and scarf in the front hall closet and went out to the kitchen.

"Um, they smell good."

She picked out a bulgy snowman and bit off the head. "For someone who hates to bake cookies, you do a pretty good job."

"You know I like to do the fancy decorating part. But unfortunately the dough has to be mixed up and baked first," her mother retorted.

"Are you going old-fashioned on them the way you did on the tree this year?"

"Of course. No pinks and blues this time. Everything must be red and green."

Vickie took another cookie and wandered back to the den to look at the ceiling-high tree. It was artificial, of course, because of apartment building fire rules against real trees. But Mrs. Montgomery had scoured the stores until she found a tree that looked so real Vickie had to feel the needles to know it was not. Then she had layered the branches with long strands of tinsel and miniature ornaments. Dozens of tiny green and red lights sparkled the tinsel.

"Now *that's* a tree," Mr. Montgomery had said late

Saturday when he turned on the lights and the tree blazed with color. "If I could just look out the window and see clean white snow, I could imagine I was back in Minnesota." He had looked around at them, shaking his head regretfully. "Instead, we have to settle for heaps of dirty snow piled along cement sidewalks."

"That's why we have to have an old-fashioned tree this year," Mrs. Montgomery answered. "An ultramodern apartment in the middle of a busy city absolutely demands a Christmasy Christmas tree."

"I'm glad," Vickie broke in. "I didn't like that all-pink thing we had last year."

"Or the silver one the year before," Francine added. "It was too glittery."

"None of you said so then," Mrs. Montgomery protested, her voice hurt sounding. "I thought you liked them. You all said they were beautiful."

"They were," Francine hastily assured her. "They were beautiful, but they weren't Christmas."

"I always thought Christmas was more than just having certain colors," Mrs. Montgomery retorted.

"It is. It's about the birth of God's Son."

Mr. Montgomery's words fell into the silence. Vickie glanced at her mother, caught the questioning look on her face, and heard her father answer the question. "That's when Christmas started."

"You found that in the Bible, I suppose?" Mrs. Montgomery's question was half a statement.

He nodded, looking back at her gravely. Vickie watched them and thought about her father reading the Bible so much since buying one last summer. When he found a story he thought she would like, he read it to her. Like the one about the young man who went to sleep in the desert and dreamed he saw a ladder reaching to heaven with angels going up and down it. And one about a wide sea where the water piled up on each side and a lot of people walked across without their feet getting wet. That one sounded like a fairy story, but her father said it was true because it was in the Bible.

Vickie wandered through the apartment, looking at the decorations in the other rooms. Her mother had crocheted little elfin figures as doorknob covers, hung mistletoe from each chandelier, outlined the wide mirror in the hall with greenery, and banked pine branches along the back of the long, polished buffet in the dining room. Though reminders of Christmas were in every room, nothing was overdone.

She went into her room to change clothes and saw the Christmas touches there too. Little straw baskets filled with red velvet bells swung from the drapery rods, a scarlet splash against the frilly white curtains. A row of carved olive wood camels marched across the dresser.

The camels reminded Vickie of the manger scene that friends had brought her from Switzerland one year when she was little. The figures were roughly carved purposely, so the friends had said. They included a little stable, the figures of Joseph and Mary, a small wooden bed for the baby, and several sheep. Two shepherds leaned on long sticks that were curved at the top. The friends had sounded embarrassed when they said the manger scene was supposed to picture God sending His Son to be born in a stable and that it should be a part of every Christmas celebration.

Vickie remembered how she had listened without understanding and how her parents had seemed embarrassed and were not able to explain it any better. She had been six that year, and her mother had let her put the figures by the wall, next to the tree. They had quickly been hidden by a mound of presents and then, after Christmas, packed away. She had not seen them since. But if this was to be an old-fashioned Christmas, then this was the year to get out the manger scene.

"Icings are ready, Vickie."

"OK. Let me call Diane. I promise not to talk."

She dialed and listened to the phone ring in the empty-sounding apartment. Diane and her mother must have decided to stay downtown and eat. She hung up the phone and went out to the kitchen.

"What's this wrapped in foil?"

"A loaf of Anna's Christmas bread. The recipe belonged to her 'mama's mama's mama' she said."

"I thought she'd still be here when I got home. Did you give her my present?"

"Yes. She came early today because—Ooops!" Mrs. Montgomery bent to snatch a pan of cookies from the oven. "I would hate to burn this last batch. Move those over so there is room for these to cool."

Vickie took another cookie and asked, "Mom, where is that little manger scene I had a long time ago?"

Her mother carefully traced a green line down each limb of a cookie tree, her hand steady on a thin paint brush, the tip of her tongue showing the way it did when she concentrated on an intricate painting.

Without looking around, she answered, "You mean those funny little figures the Chapmans brought you from some place? Switzerland, I think it was."

"Yeah."

"I don't know. I suppose they are packed away somewhere. What made you think of them?"

"I guess maybe because of what Dad said. You know—about the story in the Bible."

"Oh." Her mother's hand was motionless for a moment. Then she shrugged. "I'm afraid we gave most of your old toys away."

"But those weren't toys," Vickie protested. She could not explain even to herself why they seemed so important. "Think we can find them?"

"We can look in the storage room tomorrow. But let's get these cookies finished now."

When they had the frosted cookies stored away, Vickie helped make an omelet and fix a salad for supper. Sitting at the table by the plant-filled window always reminded her of the SOS signs in Diane's window last summer, the first step in their discovering each other. Now Diane was a closer friend than the girls she had known from sandbox days.

Vickie looked out past the soft glow of the electric candles her mother had put on the marble window sills in each room. She had saved a white iced snowman to eat with a dish of peppermint ice cream, and they ate dessert by the glow of the candles. As she looked across the courtyard at the other building, lights flashed in Diane's apartment.

"Oh, good! She's home."

Mrs. Montgomery looked across at the lighted windows and then asked, "What are your plans for vacation? Besides sleeping late and doing nothing," she added, a teasing laugh coloring her voice.

"I don't know. I'm going to call Diane and ask what she wants to do."

A tiny frown puckered the smooth skin between her mother's eyebrows as she said, "Why not invite some of your old friends in for a slumber party after Christmas? Or, you might want to visit them for a few days. You've scarcely seen Betty Lou or Pam or Sandy since school started. In fact, not since—since we moved here."

Vickie heard the slight hesitation in her mother's voice and knew she had really meant to say, "Not since you and Diane became friends."

And that was true. In the last five months she and Diane had become inseparable. But there were lots of reasons for that. They were the only ones the same age in either building. They went to the same school, had the same teachers and the same assignments. They liked to do the same things.

But there was more to it than that. Diane was part of the now of her life. Betty Lou and Sandy and Pam belonged to a past that seemed remote and unreal, a past she was no longer part of.

She thought back to the weekend she had visited Betty Lou right after school started. Sandy had been there too. It was fun at first to be with her best friends again and do the things she had done before they had moved to the city. But after the first few hours of talking and laughing, she had found herself just a listener. She had sat on the fringe while Betty Lou and Sandy talked about people she did not know. They were not the least bit interested in her life. She tried to tell them about herself and Diane, about how different apartment living was, and how much fun it was to take a city bus to school instead of walking. They listened with polite inattention and then went right back to talking about themselves. She had felt "out of it" all weekend.

Mother did not seem to understand and kept talking about how she should make other friends. But Diane was the only one around. And she was more fun than a bunch of friends.

"Vickie?" her mother prompted, waiting for an answer.

"Yeah, but maybe no one will want to come."

"Of course they will! They are probably as eager for

12

something different to do as you are. Why not call Betty Lou and ask? If she can't come for an overnight visit, at least invite her in for a day."

Vickie sighed. Her mother was determined to get her back in touch so she might as well go along with it. Maybe if Betty Lou and Sandy came here they would not talk so much about themselves. And she could invite Diane too.

"Okay, I'll ask them. But I want to call Diane in a minute and see how she got along at the doctor."

"Was this just a routine checkup?"

"Well, not exactly. She was hoping he would take the cast off today. She was supposed to wear it four months and it's been that almost."

Mrs. Montgomery looked at Vickie and said slowly, "Anna expressed concern over Diane when she came to clean today. She said, 'That one is too thin and she is hurting.'"

"Yeah, I'm sure her back bothers her a lot, but she gets mad if anyone asks her about it. She doesn't want anyone to know she wears a cast."

"I think Anna was referring more to her spirit than to her body," Mrs. Montgomery answered.

"What do you mean?"

After a minute her mother answered, her voice careful, "I don't see Diane very often. She doesn't come here as often as you go there. I must admit that bothers me a little. Is there any reason for it?"

"No." Vickie shrugged. "Whenever I suggest coming here, she says let's stay at her house. She's got so many books and games and stuff. And her mother is gone a lot."

She looked across at her mother and added defensively, "We don't do anything we shouldn't."

"I'm not for a moment suggesting that you do. It just seems to me that Diane is a very alone person, especially

13

since she does not have a happy family life. I think that's partly what Anna means."

"Maybe Anna doesn't see her fun side like I do."

Her mother nodded. "Perhaps not. Perhaps she knows she doesn't have to show only that side to Anna."

Vickie puzzled over the remark as she moved one of the phones into her room and dialed Diane's number. When Diane answered, she could tell from the discouraged droop in her voice that the doctor's report was not good.

"He said my back is healing a lot slower than he thought it would. I've got to wear the dumb old cast a lot longer. At least a couple of months."

"That isn't too bad—"

"Sure! You're not wearing it! And he said still no sports next semester. None at all."

Vickie knew it would not help to remind Diane that she had known that all along and had just pretended she would be able to play volleyball. Not knowing how to make Diane feel better, she said, "Hey, how about coming over for a while? I've got to invite Betty Lou and Sandy for an overnight, and we can talk about it."

She listened to the silence on the line. Then Diane asked, "How come you have to invite them?"

"Oh, it's really my mother's idea. She thinks I'm not paying enough attention to my old friends."

"You'd better do it. She likes them better than she does me."

"Don't be silly!" Vickie protested, hearing her voice come a little too quick and loud. "Anyway, I want you to come too."

"I can't. I'll be busy."

"How do you know that when you don't know when I'm going to invite them? I'll make it a time you're not busy. What day next week shall I ask them?"

After another stretch of silence, Diane's voice came back with a chilly, hostile sound Vickie had not heard in it before.

"Invite them any time you want to. I don't care." Then, before Vickie could protest, she said, "Look, I've got to hang up. My mother is expecting a call."

"But—" Vickie said to the click of the receiver.

She sat staring at the phone, still hearing the forlorn sound in Diane's voice. She must have had a really rough time at the doctor. She had so much counted on getting the cast off even though she would still have to be careful about doing things. No wonder she sounded grouchy, so unlike her usual sparkling self.

But all evening the cold sound of Diane's voice rang in her ears. Was it the idea of the overnight with Betty Lou and Sandy that upset her? She did hate anyone's seeing the cast that covered her like a vest from under her arms to down over her hips. She hated anyone's asking about it, hated sympathy about anything. Maybe that partly explained Anna's words.

"Well, then, I'll wait until she gets the cast off before having the girls in for an overnight. Diane is more important to me right now than Betty Lou and Sandy are. She *needs* my friendship."

2

The shrill ring of the phone woke Vickie and she sat up, yawning. Then she threw back the covers and felt for her slippers. Maybe that was Diane, feeling better in the cold morning sunshine and with an idea of something fun to do.

But the ringing stopped before she reached the kitchen extension, and she heard her mother's light, lilting voice in the den.

"Hello? Thelma! How nice to hear from you."

Vickie made a face. Betty Lou's mother. "They probably want me to come to their house during vacation," she muttered.

Then she heard shock deepening her mother's voice as Mrs. Montgomery said, "Oh, I'm so sorry."

Vickie went into the den to listen as her mother went on. "Why, of course, she can come here. Vickie and I were talking just last night about inviting her for a visit . . . Is there anything else we can do? . . Don't worry about Betty Lou. We'll try to make Christmas as happy as possible for her . . . And let us know how Jack gets along. If there are any legal complications, let Carl know. He will be glad to help."

"What's wrong?" Vickie stared at the sober expression on her mother's face as she put down the receiver.

"Betty Lou's father is out west on a business trip and was seriously injured in an auto accident early this morning. He's in a hospital there, and Thelma is flying out to be with him. Betty Lou could stay with Sandy or one of the other neighbors, but her mother thought it would be better if she had a complete change of circumstances. Since you girls are such good friends, she thought right away of us."

"Oh, sure. It'll be fun having her."

And this would solve the problem that had bothered her last night. Diane would understand why Betty Lou had to come. It would not be the same as actually inviting someone to stay over. And maybe she and Betty Lou could get back their old familiar friendship and not seem like strangers to each other. This would be a super way to introduce an old best friend to a new best friend.

"When is she coming?"

"This afternoon. Thelma just got word of the accident an hour ago. I said we would drive out and get Betty Lou, but a friend is driving Thelma to the airport and they are coming early enough to bring her."

Vickie followed her mother as she went to the linen closet and pulled out sheets and towels, saying, "It's fortunate we kept the twin beds for your room. Betty Lou will be here at least a week and possibly for all Christmas vacation, depending on how her father gets along."

"I'm sorry her dad got hurt, but I'm really glad she's coming."

Vickie's enthusiasm made her gulp down a quick breakfast and dash over to Diane's to blurt out the news. She found Diane sitting cross-legged on her bedroom floor, absorbed in making a macrame plant holder for her mother's Christmas present. She listened to Vickie's breathless explanation as she carefully tied knots. A frown of concentration drew her eyebrows together.

When she did not say anything, Vickie went on. "The

three of us can have a lot of fun."

Her voice sounded loud, and she knew she was trying to make Diane believe something she was not really sure of herself.

"Uh-huh." Diane's slender fingers twisted and pulled and tied the long strings. She stopped occasionally to study the directions.

"You'll like Betty Lou." Vickie hurried out the words. "She's really nice. And a lot of fun."

"Is she always called that?"

"What? Betty Lou? Sure. It's her name. Why?"

Diane shrugged. "Just wondered. We had neighbors once whose little girl had that name. She was about two."

She looked up at Vickie briefly and then bent her head again and carefully tied another knot.

Vickie said the name to herself several times. It did sound babyish. Then she was angry at herself for thinking that. She and Betty Lou had been friends for a long time. She took a deep breath to protest and then stopped. Maybe Diane had not meant it that way at all. And anyway, she would change her mind about Betty Lou when she got to know her.

But the more Vickie thought about it, the less sure she was. Diane was really acting funny about Betty Lou's coming, and she could not figure out why. They had other friends in school and they all fooled around together. Why was Betty Lou any different? She kept thinking about it as she fussed about her room in the afternoon, shoving over the clothes in the closet and emptying a couple of drawers for Betty Lou's stuff.

When Betty Lou came, her mother stopped only long enough for a quick, "Thanks so much. I'll call when I have news," before hurrying away.

"Thanks for letting me come. I didn't want to stay with

18

anyone in the neighborhood where I'd see our house every day and think about Dad and—and wonder how he was."

Betty Lou's voice quavered as she finished the sentence. Mrs. Montgomery smiled at her. "Well, the place is different from our house where you always felt at home, but we're the same family you have always known so you should not feel like a stranger."

At dinner, Betty Lou sat open-mouthed, listening to Francine spill out the funny and interesting things in her day.

"I've seen you lots of times on TV."

"If you've seen me *lots,* I must have a twin." Francine laughed as she looked back at the admiration in Betty Lou's eyes. "I'm not on as often as I'd like to be. Mostly I just do routine things—looking up stuff in the files for other people to report on."

Mr. Montgomery looked at Francine, the smile on his lips reflecting in his eyes. "Pete wishes you were on television a whole lot less than you are. He would like to put you somewhere else permanently."

Francine looked at her father, her eyes troubled. "He *is* getting persistent," she answered. "He wants to give me something for Christmas that I'm not ready for quite yet."

"Don't accept it unless you are absolutely sure," her father warned.

Vickie looked from one to the other, knowing they were talking about an engagement ring, and wondering why Francine would even think of refusing Pete.

"Who is Pete?" Betty Lou asked as they got ready for bed.

"The guy she's going with. He saw her do an interview on TV. You know, one of those human interest things where they go out and talk to someone. It was the first one she had done, and she was really nervous. She thought she'd messed it up, but Pete was really impressed."

"You mean she interviewed him?"

"No. He just happened to catch the program. Then he went to the studio to meet her. He kept going back until she finally agreed to go out to lunch with him. That did it for her, and they've been dating ever since."

"Are they going to get married?"

Vickie shook her head. "I don't know, but I hope so. He's really a terrrific guy."

She and Betty Lou lay in bed a long time talking, and it was just the way it had always been between them, easy, comfortable talking with lots of laughs.

Because they talked so long, they were late getting up. While they ate breakfast, Vickie told Betty Lou about the signals Diane had put in her window last summer and the mystery she had imagined because of them.

"Here Diane was just trying to get my attention, and I built up a big case about it being a little kidnapped boy asking for help. Really dumb of me—"

She stopped abruptly. "Oh, no! I forgot—Diane and I were going shopping today!"

She dashed to the phone, dialed, and listened to it ring repeatedly.

"Diane must have gone without waiting for us," she said regretfully over her shoulder.

She started to hang up and then heard the receiver lift. "Hello?"

"Oh, Diane! I was afraid you'd gone. Why didn't you remind me about this yesterday?"

After a slight pause, Diane said, "I didn't think you needed a reminder. You never have before."

"I wouldn't have this time, but Betty Lou and I were so busy hashing over things, that I forgot."

As soon as she said the words, she wanted to snatch

them back. That was the wrong thing to say with Diane acting so funny about Betty Lou's visit.

Diane's voice was frosty. "Since you're so busy today, you don't have to bother going with me."

"I want to," Vickie interrupted. "And Betty Lou does too. We can meet you in ten minutes."

"You won't be through with your breakfast by then."

"How did you know—? Oh." Vickie broke off the sentence. The binoculars again. Diane had promised last summer that she would not use them that way anymore.

"We'll meet you by the fountain in ten minutes," she insisted.

"If you want to." Diane's voice was still cold, almost sullen.

"I do want to" Vickie replied firmly, and waited.

Diane was silent again. Then, unexpectedly, the sparkle flashed in her voice as she answered, "OK. See you in ten minutes."

Vickie let her breath out in a sigh of relief. Everything was going to be all right after all. She gulped the rest of her cocoa standing up and piled her dishes in a heap as she talked. "I'll tell my mother we're going while you brush your teeth and stuff. But we'll have to leave in a couple of minutes."

The studio door was closed, but the No Admittance sign was gone. Mrs. Montgomery always packed away her painting to keep special holiday times like Christmas free for family activities.

Vickie tapped on the door and opened it. "We're going. Got to hurry to meet Diane. We'll get a hamburger downtown for lunch."

"Have a good time, girls. Remember, mothers get special presents." She smiled at them. Then she added, "Oh, Vickie, one present I haven't gotten your father yet is

21

his yearly puzzle. Try to find him a really mammoth one, will you please? Find one hard enough to keep him working for a few hours."

The elevator was unusually long in coming, and when it finally did, it stopped at almost every floor. When they pushed through the lobby's revolving doors, Vickie peered through the frosted glass. She could see impatience in Diane's figure as she stood kicking one foot against the low wall around the fountain.

"Hi," Vickie said breathlessly. "That elevator! I've never seen it so slow. This is Betty Lou. And this is Diane."

She looked from one to the other and relaxed when she saw Diane smile at Betty Lou. Apparently she had let her mind worry overtime, imagining a problem that did not exist. It was silly to think Diane would not like Betty Lou. They caught a bus almost immediately, crowded on, and worked their way toward the back. By the time they got to the back door, they were at their stop and hurried off the bus and into the store out of the cold.

Diane looked at Vickie. "Well, what shall we do? Just go separately for what we're buying or stick together?"

"I'm not buying anything," Betty Lou answered. "So I'll just tag along with one of you. With you, Vickie," she added quickly.

"I'm supposed to get my dad a puzzle. Just for kicks," she hastily explained to the surprise in Diane's raised eyebrows. "My mother gets him one every year for Christmas because that's the only time he likes to fool around working one."

"Well, I've got to buy a couple of presents and I sure could use some advice. Vickie, why don't you get your Dad's puzzle and then meet Betty Lou and me."

"Okay. Where?"

"I've got to buy my grandmother some embroidery stuff. I'll get that last and we can meet there. Second floor, my mother said."

"Okay," Vickie agreed, looking away from the appeal in Betty Lou's eyes that they stay together. Diane's suggestion was great. It would give the two of them a chance to get to know each other. And it would make Diane see that Betty Lou's visit would not change their friendship at all.

"Okay, you guys," she said again. "See you in about forty-five minutes. And then let's eat. I'm already starved."

When Vickie got to the toy floor, she detoured to watch the electric trains whizzing around tracks set in a roped-off section. By the time she bought the puzzle and got down on the escalator from the fifth to the second floor, an hour had gone by. She elbowed her way through the crowds to the needlework section and saw Diane and Betty Lou by a counter piled high with skeins of yarn. Vickie hurried toward them. Just then a man, who had been standing on the side watching the shoppers, stepped up to Betty Lou.

"Stay right where you are, girls," Vickie heard him say.

They turned to look at him, and other people shopping nearby stopped, too, listening curiously.

He looked at Betty Lou. "Will you please open your bag?"

He motioned at the colorful Christmas shopping bag she carried. Betty Lou stared up at him in bewilderment, and Diane asked, "Why?"

He ignored her and continued to look sternly at Betty Lou. "If you don't open it voluntarily, I shall have to do it for you." He pulled back his coat and reached into an inside pocket. "I'm the store detective."

Betty Lou looked scared and embarrassed. People were

stopping to watch and listen, but the detective waved them away. Betty Lou put down the bag and pulled the handles apart. She stared at something in the bag and then looked up at him.

"But where—how—how did this stuff get in here?"

She reached and pulled out two large soft skeins of scarlet yarn and stood holding them, looking helplessly from Vickie to the detective and then at the yarn.

"I-I d-don't know how they g-got in there." Her voice stumbled in embarrassment. "I didn't take them. I wouldn't *do* anything like that."

"She wouldn't!" Vickie broke in, her voice loud and positive.

And Diane said, "You must be mistaken."

"Then how do you explain the fact that they are in her bag—unwrapped?"

"Well—they must—they could just have fallen in," Diane suggested. We were looking at all the stuff on the counter. The bag was on the floor. Some of it must have got knocked off, and we didn't notice."

"That's very unlikely," he replied, his voice and face stern and unyielding.

"But it *could* have happened that way. It must have." Diane's face was upturned to him, her voice pleading.

He looked from her to Betty Lou, then to Vickie, and back again to Diane. "Do you know her well?" he asked abruptly.

Diane hesitated. She licked her lips with the tip of her tongue and darted a pleading look at Vickie. "Well—no. We—you see, she and I just met, but—"

Vickie broke in swiftly. "I know her. And she would never, never, never steal anything."

He put the yarn back on the counter and looked at Betty Lou. "I will give you the benefit of the doubt this time. But just remember that what you did is called shoplifting, and it is a crime that is punishable by law."

"But I didn't—" Betty Lou began, tears standing in her eyes.

"Come on, Betty Lou. Let's go eat."

Vickie was so angry she was shaking as she took Betty Lou's arm. "Don't worry. *We* know you didn't do it." She hurried her toward the escalator. "Don't worry about what he thinks."

But Betty Lou only shook her head miserably, not looking at anyone. They rode the escalator to the sixth floor and Betty Lou held a table while Vickie and Diane stood in line to order hamburgers. When they brought the food, Betty Lou did not touch the french fries and only ate a couple of bites of the hamburger.

Going home on the bus, Vickie automatically slid into a seat with Betty Lou, leaving Diane to ride by herself. She could not think of anything to say to cheer up Betty Lou and could only hope that this would not spoil the whole vacation. How awful for this to happen to Betty Lou when she was already feeling bad about her father and about not being home for Christmas. She and Diane would have to come up with fun things to do in the next few days.

When they got off the bus and walked the short block to the apartment, Diane stopped by the fountain and turned impulsively.

"Let's do lots of fun stuff together," she said, her breath coming in frosty puffs in the cold air. "We can start right now. My mother won't be home from work till late, so how about coming over? We can play games and stuff." She looked at them, her face alive with eagerness.

"Great," Vickie answered quickly. Lots of activity would help Betty Lou forget the embarrassment.

25

"Come as soon after dinner as you can," Diane called after them.

As she thought about the evening, Vickie was glad Mrs. Stewart would not be home. She never felt really comfortable around Diane's mother even though she was always friendly.

Mrs. Stewart was nice but brittle. That was the word Francine had used about her last summer when Mrs. Montgomery had invited Diane and her mother over for dinner. Vickie had not seen it at the time. But in the almost six months she and Diane had been friends, she had often wondered how Diane could be so sparkly and warm when her mother usually said sarcastic, unkind things about people.

She remembered that her mother had answered Francine, "Perhaps we would be cynical too if we had gone through what she has."

Vickie had looked up the word *cynical* and found it meant distrustful of others. Maybe being divorced had made her brittle and cynical. Anyway, Diane was not like that.

But she is acting different now, a voice deep inside reminded her. Diane had certainly been cold at the thought of Betty Lou's coming. Still—she had not acted that way in the store. She had been the one to really stand up for Betty Lou.

3

At dinner, Vickie's parents listened sympathetically as she and Betty Lou spilled out what had happened in the store.

"Why didn't the detective believe her?" Vickie demanded. "How could he just keep insisting that Betty Lou was a thief?"

"That's what circumstantial evidence is, girls," Mr. Montgomery answered. "The yarn *was* in your shopping bag unwrapped—"

"But I didn't put it there," Betty Lou broke in defensively. "In fact, it wasn't even mine. The shopping bag, I mean. Diane bought it for all her stuff, and I was just holding it for her while she tried to decide what to buy for her grandmother."

Mr. Montgomery nodded in sympathy as he answered, "But you see, the store detective couldn't overlook the fact that the yarn was in your bag and that someone must have put it there. Since he didn't know that you wouldn't steal, he had to assume that you had taken it. His first responsibility is to protect the store."

"But no one put the yarn in the bag," Vickie objected. "Only Diane and Betty Lou were there. Nobody else was even standing near them. So what Diane said must be right—that it just fell in."

Her father raised his shoulders in a shrug. "That would not ordinarily happen, so you must not blame the man for

27

doubting you. Don't be hard on him for just doing his job."

"The worst thing is that he didn't believe me. I felt so awful! Everybody looked at me. I'll never go in that store again."

Betty Lou looked around the table at them, blinking hard to keep back tears. Her voice was small and tight. "If I could, I'd go home right now. But I can't, because no one is there."

Mrs. Montgomery got up for more coffee and put her arm quickly and lightly around Betty Lou's shoulders as she passed her. "You aren't in a strange place as long as you are with us." She shook her head, laughter coloring her voice. "Just remember how many times you and Vickie were not sure which place was home when you were little, your house or ours. When you are with us, you *are* home."

"And we'll have fun tonight," Vickie reassured her. She looked at her mother. "Diane invited us over. Her mother is going someplace right after work and she'll be all alone. OK?"

She caught the quick exchange of glances between her parents before her mother answered, "All right. But come home at ten o'clock."

Vickie and Betty Lou cleared the dinner table while the Montgomerys sat talking over dessert and coffee. Vickie could hear snatches of their low-voiced conversation, her mother saying, ". . . probably going to an office party. I wish I had suggested Diane come here in case Mrs. Stewart is not—" She stopped and then finished, "Is not feeling well when she gets home."

And her father replied, "We cannot interfere too much. Though I am certain we must talk to Vickie about the situation sometime soon."

"Perhaps we should wait until the holidays are over and the girls are back in school. It may be that Diane will feel better in the spring. Her back problem must cause great pressures for her along with the other situations."

Vickie silently agreed. Anyone who had scoliosis could be forgiven for being grouchy once in a while. But she wondered what else they were talking about. What other situations did they mean?

When she and Betty Lou got to the apartment, Diane was waiting for them with a stack of games and a card table set up in her bedroom by the window.

"Take your pick," she said to Betty Lou with a sweep of her arm over the games. "You're the visitor so you choose first."

"Monopoly," Betty Lou answered promptly.

"OK. But I'm the champ at that game," Diane warned. "I always win no matter who plays."

And she did, though Betty Lou was a close second. After playing Monopoly and a couple of games of Chinese checkers, Diane stood up.

"Let's eat. Vickie, come help me."

"I'll put this stuff away," Betty Lou offered.

"OK. The games go on my closet shelf over there. We'll get the food and bring it in here."

Vickie helped Diane pull out boxes of pretzels and corn chips and cookies, and spread cheese on crackers. They piled it on a tray and carried it and bottles of Coke to the bedroom where Betty Lou stood looking out the window.

She turned around. "These apartments are so neat! I looked in at your mother's room. It's so pretty. It looks like a picture in one of those how-to-decorate magazines my mother buys."

Diane shrugged. "She bought all new furniture for her room when we moved here. Since she was buying only for herself, she got the kind of stuff she likes."

Vickie shot a quick glance at Betty Lou, relieved to see that she apparently had not really listened to what Diane said. She watched Diane pile food on a plate and asked, "Didn't you eat any supper?"

"Just a peanut butter sandwich. I didn't want to bother cooking. Anyway, I ate all Betty Lou's french fries at lunch."

"You could have come over and eaten with us."

"No." Diane's voice was abrupt and angry sounding and her face had a closed-off look that bothered Vickie. Something was definitely bothering Diane, and it must be more than just the scoliosis and more than Betty Lou's being here.

Then Diane changed again, doing an imitation of the man who had taken their hamburger order, and doubling them over with laughter. When Vickie finally looked at her watch, she exclaimed, "Hey, we've got to go."

"Not already," Diane begged. "It's early yet."

"My mother said ten o'clock. You know by now that when she *suggests* a time, she *means* that time."

"Does she still lop off from the next deadline the minutes you miss on one before?" Betty Lou asked.

When Vickie nodded, Betty Lou laughed. "Remember all the times you missed whole days because we overstayed your deadlines so many times?"

Vickie's laugh in return disappeared when she glanced at Diane. The expression on her face was hard as she stared sullenly at Betty Lou. But she could understand Diane's feelings. Here she was with a hurting back, left alone in an empty apartment, while two friends went off to share a room and laugh together at memories of past fun.

She said quickly, "I'll call you first thing tomorrow.

You come over and we'll do things."

"Maybe."

Diane's voice was curt again, and she stood with folded arms watching them pull on their jackets. She did not walk to the elevator with them, but instead closed the door hard.

The elevator came quickly and plummeted them to the ground floor. The doors slid open, and they could hear loud voices as they got off the elevator. They crossed the marble floor to the lobby and stopped. People stood watching a woman in a long beige mink coat arguing with the doorman. She swayed unsteadily on her feet, a chiffon scarf dragging on the marble floor. Her voice slurred as she talked, calling him names.

Charlie answered her quietly and held the door open for her. His voice was gentle as he said, "Let me help you to the elevator."

She jerked her arm from his touch. "Leave me 'lone. I know m'way home. You think I'm drunk. Well, I'm not. Never been drunk in m'life. My ex-husband got drunk. I never do."

The scarf dragged and the mink slipped from one shoulder as she walked unsteadily toward the bank of elevators.

Betty Lou turned to stare after her. "Wow! Is she drunk!"

But Vickie turned her head away and pulled the hood of her jacket close around her face. She fumbled for her mittens in her jacket pocket and pulled Betty Lou along. "Come on, let's go."

She felt sick. She had never seen Diane's mother like this, looking sloppy. Every other time she had seen Mrs. Stewart, at home or going to and coming from work, she had been immaculate. She was very fussy about her

31

clothes. Vickie remembered Diane's once showing her her mother's closet with its stacks of see-through boxes of shoes and purses and even hats.

She had exclaimed, "Your mother has more clothes than my mother and Francine put together." Diane had shrugged. She said, her voice indifferent, "My mother's clothes are part of the settlement." Though she had not asked, Vickie supposed that meant Diane's father still paid the bills for Mrs. Stewart's clothes.

As Vickie hurried Betty Lou across the lobby and out into the courtyard, she was glad Diane's mother had not recognized her. She did not want Mrs. Stewart to know she had seen her looking and talking like that. It was a good thing they had left before Mrs. Stewart got to the apartment. Diane would have been so embarrassed to have them see her mother in that condition. She hoped when Diane came over that Betty Lou would not talk about the drunk they had seen. Just thinking the word in connection with Diane's mother was awful.

Of course lots of people they knew drank. Her parents did once in a while, at parties. But she knew her mother usually asked for ginger ale and her father held his cocktail a whole evening, only sipping a little now and then. She thought of the conversation she had overheard after dinner. When her parents talked about Mrs. Stewart not being well when she came home from the party, this must be what they had meant.

She lay awake a long time after Betty Lou went to sleep, thinking about Diane. And her mother. And her father. How awful it must be to have your parents divorced. Diane had never talked about her father in the six months they had been friends, even though they talked about everything else. Vickie wondered what he looked like. There were no pictures of him in the apartment, and in the album Diane had shown her, blank spaces gaped where there once had been pictures. She thought Diane must look like him because she did not look like her mother. Their hair was the same silky gold color, but their faces were different.

Boy, am I lucky to have parents who love each other! The thought gradually stopped her whirling thoughts, and she fell asleep.

The phone rang the next morning just as they were getting up, and Vickie went yawning to the living room phone. Diane's voice was shot through with excitement and dismay.

"Vickie, guess what! You know those antique gold bracelets my mother has? Remember I showed them to you once? Well, they've disappeared. She can't find them anyplace."

Vickie yawned. She could not get excited about it when she felt drugged from lack of sleep.

"Maybe she just put them someplace else and forgot where."

Diane's voice showed her impatience at the suggestion. "No, they aren't anyplace. She hunted for them last night when she came home, and they are gone."

Vickie came wide awake at that, last night's picture of Mrs. Stewart vivid in her mind. Last night Mrs. Stewart could not have found anything even if it was in plain sight. She said carefully, "Maybe if she looks today—"

"I've been up for hours looking, and I can't find them either," Diane interrupted. "The thing is, my grandmother is coming for her usual Christmas visit. She'll be here Saturday. One of the first things she always asks about is those bracelets. They're more important to her than *anything*. They've been in the family for centuries. My grandmother is always sure that those would be the first things a burglar would take. And now they have been."

"Is anything else missing?"

"I don't think so. But nothing else matters. It's the bracelets my mother is worried about."

"I suppose they're expensive."

"Yeah. But mostly it's because they're old that they're valuable. They were given to my great-something-or-other by someone famous."

"Has your mother called the police?"

"Oh, no." Diane's voice was quick. Then she added, "Not yet, anyway. Not until we've looked some more."

"Can I do anything? Help look?"

"How could you find them if we can't?"

Vickie pulled the phone away from her ear at the loud, sharp sound in Diane's voice. She was sure making a lot out of nothing. Mrs. Stewart had probably stuck them away once when she was—Vickie shied away from the word that was in her mind.

Then Diane's voice softened again as she asked, "Is it all right if I come over? My mother isn't going to work today. She has a—a bad headache so she's still in bed. It's kind of boring over here."

Vickie tried to keep the surprise out of her voice as she answered, "Sure. Great!" And she thought, *This should make Mom happy, since Diane is coming here.*

"Hey, Vickie." Diane's voice sounded embarrassed. "Don't—don't say anything to anyone about the bracelets being gone, okay? To Betty Lou—or anyone?"

"It won't matter to her."

"I know. But I don't want to talk about it."

"OK. I won't say anything."

Vickie put down the receiver and stood by the phone for a moment, wondering. How could a burglar have gotten into the apartment and taken only those bracelets? Diane was probably just covering for her mother, not wanting to admit that her mother had not known what she was doing the last time she had put them away. Poor Diane. Anna was right to worry about her.

Vickie went back to the bedroom where Betty Lou was sitting in the middle of the bed, looking at an old scrapbook.

"Diane's coming to eat with us."

"What did you say was wrong with her back?"

"Scoliosis. It's something that twists your spine all crooked and can really be serious if it isn't corrected. She had to have an operation and now she has to wear this cast. She was hoping she'd get it off during this vacation. But the doctor told her Tuesday that it wouldn't come off for a couple of months yet."

"Does it hurt? The sco—whatever."

"She never talks about it, but I know it bothers her more than she lets on."

Vickie went into the bathroom to brush her teeth. Talking over the sound of the running water, her mouth full of toothpaste, she said, "Diane is a lot of fun, and she's *so* smart. She never has to study, and she remembers practically everything she reads. Our science teacher calls her a walking encyclopedia."

"She sure has lots of books. I thought you did, but she has tons more. Does she have brothers and sisters?"

"No. She's like you—a spoiled only child." Vickie laughed and ducked out of reach of the towel Betty Lou snapped at her.

"What are her parents like?"

The picture came back of Mrs. Stewart swaying unsteadily on her feet, her voice thick and rough. Vickie pulled a sweater over her head, muffling her voice as she answered, "Oh, her mother's nice." Then she added quickly, "Let's go eat. I'm hungry."

They went to the kitchen and saw the wreath-shaped paper propped against the toaster. Vickie picked up the note and skimmed it.

"I thought the house sounded quiet. My mother's shopping. She said to help ourselves but not make a mess and not make a whole breakfast out of Christmas cookies."

"She still sounds like my mother," Betty Lou replied. "Anyway, I only want cereal."

"OK. Then let's eat here in the kitchen instead of lugging everything into the dining room. Get the spoons and stuff from the drawer there, will you, while I let Diane in," Vickie said as she went to the door.

"Yikes, it's cold out there," Diane said as she came in, unzipping her hooded jacket. "I'll bet the wind chill factor is about fifty below."

Vickie laughed at Betty Lou and lifted her shoulders in an exaggerated gesture. "See what I mean? She's up on all the current stuff."

"All you have to do is listen to weather reports," Diane retorted. "Can I dump my jacket in your bedroom?"

"Sure, but it's a mess. We just got up."

Vickie followed Diane and stood in the doorway watching her drop her jacket and mittens on a chair and then lean to dig into the jacket pocket.

"Have you got a Kleenex around?" she asked over her shoulder. "I thought I had some, but there's so much stuff in my pocket—"

"You always carry more junk around with you!" Vickie exclaimed. She explained to Betty Lou. "It's really crazy to go out for a walk with her. She picks up stones and pieces of tree branches and leaves and bird feathers and brings them home to look at under the microscope."

She looked at Diane. "What did you find just between your apartment and mine to make your pocket so bulgy?"

She pretended to grab for the jacket, but Diane fended her off, clutching it against herself.

"If you must know, snoopy, it's your Christmas present. I was going to stick it under the tree without your knowing it."

"You mean my present is so small you can put it in your pocket?" Vickie pretended mock anger and then said, "I'm kidding."

Diane half turned to shield what she was doing. When she turned around, she held a narrow box wrapped in silver paper and tied with a puff of pale blue ribbon.

"Where's your tree?"

She followed Vickie and Betty Lou into the den and stopped, staring at the ceiling-high tree.

"Oh." Her voice showed her surprised dismay. "I thought your mother would have a blue and silver tree to match the rest of your house, and that's why I wrapped your present like this. Instead she's gone all red and green like all the rest of us."

She squatted awkwardly in front of the tree. "I'll shove your present in the back so the unmatched colors won't show and where you won't pick it up and shake it."

Then she saw the manger scene that Vickie had arranged on a low table next to the fireplace. "What's this?" She picked up the Joseph figure and turned him around in her hands, running her fingers over the beard and down the long fold of his robe. Then she saw the two roughly carved shepherd figures.

As she looked up at Vickie, her eyes lit with her affectionate, teasing smile. "You really are going all out for Christmas, aren't you? Where'd you get these?"

"Oh, I've had them since I was little. Some friends of my

37

parents were in Switzerland one summer. They stopped in a store and saw an old man carving them."

"How come he didn't do a better job? Look how bumpy the figures are. And the baby looks kind of dumb. I saw some figures in the dime store that were better than these. I'll bet your friends got rooked and paid a lot more for them than they're worth."

Her voice was contemptuous. She dropped the figures she had picked up. Joseph fell against one of the shepherd figures and knocked it over.

Vickie looked down at the manger scene and found herself swept by anger. What right did Diane have to make fun of it just because she did not like it? It was none of her business.

"They're *supposed* to look like this."

Her voice was cold as she stooped to set the shepherd upright and adjust the tiny baby figure in the manger. She knew her mother thought the figures were toys that did not fit the other Christmas decorations, and that did not bother her too much. But Diane's scorn made her angry and stiffened her liking for the little figures. A manger scene *did* belong in Christmas. The friends had explained the meaning when they gave it to her.

When she straightened up, Betty Lou whispered, "I think the figures are darling."

Diane had gone back to the bedroom for another Kleenex and came out wiping her nose, which was red from her cold. She looked from Vickie to Betty Lou, standing together by the tree, and then down at the manger scene.

"Hey, I'm sorry. I didn't mean to knock something that was special to you. I guess I've just never thought of Christmas that way. As being a religious thing, I mean. Of course, I guess it really is."

She stopped and then, her voice dragging the explanation, she said, "You see, we just have never done special things for Christmas or any other time."

When Vickie heard the bleak sadness in Diane's voice and saw the regret shadowing her eyes, she could not stay angry.

She smiled back. "That's OK. Let's go eat."

4

The pile of beautifully wrapped packages under the wide-spreading branches of the Christmas tree grew every time anyone walked by it. Mr. Montgomery added a bunch of knobby, odd-shaped packages Friday evening when he came home from the office.

Francine and Vickie pounced on a couple of the most mysterious looking gifts, squeezing and shaking them.

Francine said, "I can't wait to see what's in this one, especially since it has my name on it." She looked at her mother. "Dad's gifts are things that you didn't know you wanted until, unwrapping them, you knew they were just what you'd hoped to get."

Mrs. Montgomery nodded. "Like the charm bracelet he bought me three years ago. Remember? Instead of ordinary objects, he had miniature pictures made of you girls, one for each year. It's not a bit valuable in money, but it certainly is in memories."

Before breakfast the next morning, Mrs. Montgomery opened the polished mahogany dining room table full length, ready to be set buffet style for the afternoon's open house.

"I'm so glad we're having our Christmas Eve open house even here in the city," Vickie exclaimed, feeling childish in her enthusiasm.

Every year that she could remember, their house had been full of people coming on Christmas Eve for a brief visit and a taste of the cookies and breads Mrs. Montgomery began baking early in the fall and storing in the freezer.

"You thought maybe Christmas traditions belonged only in a big house in the fancy suburbs?" Her father's voice was gently teasing as he smiled at her across the breakfast table over the rim of his coffee cup.

"I must admit that I had thought of not having open house this year," Mrs. Montgomery said. "But then I thought what a shame it would be to discard all our lovely old familiar customs just because we live in a city apartment. Besides, this is a marvelous way to get all our old friends together."

"I wish my mother and dad would be here for it." Betty Lou's voice wobbled as she spoke.

"We do, too," Mrs. Montgomery answered quickly. "After all, your mother is responsible for whatever style our open house has." Laughter brimmed her voice as she went on. "I remember how horrified she was at my plans the first year we did this. We had moved next door to you the first week of December—I think you girls were a year old. We decided the best way to get acquainted with our neighbors was to have a Christmas open house. I explained to your mother that since we were not settled in yet, I wouldn't bother doing much. I would just bake a few cookies, buy some others, and serve punch. Your mother didn't say anything, but she went home and spent the whole next week baking cookies and Christmas sweet breads, stored them in the freezer, and brought them over the day before the open house. Then I discovered that your Swedish grandfather had been a baker, and your mother had grown up with home-baked goodies. That's why the idea of serving guests store-bought cookies—especially at Christmas—had horrified her."

Mr. Montgomery nodded, "And so began a tradition—"

"And one I intend to carry on when I have a family."

Vickie looked around at Francine standing in the doorway, rubbing her eyes and yawning.

"Good morning, everyone. Just let me have a cup of coffee and some juice, and then I'll be ready to help with whatever still needs doing for tonight. Thanks to Anna, everything seems to shine and sparkle."

Mr. Montgomery cleared his throat and leaned forward to put down his coffee cup. "Before we get any further into the busyness of this day, I'd like to suggest that we begin another family tradition."

"Hear, hear!" Francine smiled across at her father.

"I know how much fun your ideas are," Betty Lou exclaimed.

Vickie watched her father twist his silver coffee spoon around in his fingers, not looking at anyone. His eyes studied the design on the spoon handle as he traced it with his thumb nail.

In the expectant silence he finally said, "I suggest that, since Christmas comes on Sunday this year, we should go to church." He looked around at them all. "After all, Sunday *is* Christmas, the actual day. Since Christmas is a religious holiday, it seems to me we ought to go to church to observe it."

Vickie looked at her father, startled. Take time out from the fun of Christmas to go to church? That would spoil the whole day!

Then she heard her mother say, a quick, bright smile on her face, "Carl, that is an excellent idea. We can certainly do it this time, even if it does not become another family tradition."

But Vickie thought she heard an uncertain note in her mother's voice under the light eagerness. Vickie knew her

42

mother listened politely when her father talked about the things he was reading in the Bible, though she did not seem really interested. But then her parents had different ideas on lots of things, and yet each one respected the other person's viewpoint. That was one of the neat things about her family.

Francine said then, "But where would we go?"

"We have several choices." He reached into his pocket and pulled out a slip of paper. "I looked up some church addresses in the phone book. I thought if it was agreeable with all of you, we could go to that large church on the boulevard since it is fairly close. We could take a taxi and not get the car out."

He looked across at Francine. "Pete might go along. We had lunch together the other day, and when I suggested this, he was interested."

Francine drew her eyebrows together in a puzzled frown. "That's funny. He didn't mention it to me when we talked about his coming here for Christmas dinner."

"I asked him not to until I had had a chance to suggest the idea to you all. And anyway, it was just an incidental matter in our conversation."

Vickie could tell that the going to church idea was not incidental in his thinking. The hesitant, almost apologetic way he spoke, so unlike the usual crispness of his voice, made her sense how important this was to him. God was becoming an important part of his life. Well, if this meant so much to him, the rest of them should go along with it, even if they were not crazy about going to church on Christmas of all days. She decided to say so.

"I think it's a good idea."

"Hey, but when will we open the presents?" Betty Lou asked.

Mr. Montgomery grinned at her, a teasing note

coloring his voice as he answered, "Why, the same time we do it any other Christmas morning, of course—before the birds are awake."

The phone rang. Francine answered in the kitchen and called, "For you, Dad. It's Anna, and from the sound of her voice something is wrong."

Mr. Montgomery went to the kitchen extension and said, "Anna? Yes, how are you?"

He stood listening. In the silence, Vickie watched her mother draw circles on the tablecloth with the handle of her coffee spoon. A tiny frown pulled Mrs. Montgomery's slender eyebrows together. She looked up, met Vickie's eyes, and stood up abruptly.

"I must get busy so we don't have to rush too much later in the day. I'm counting on you three girls for help."

Before Vickie could answer, her father came to the kitchen doorway. "Louise, Anna is in some kind of trouble, but between her tears and her angry, broken English, I'm not clear just what it is. If you'll talk to her on this phone, I'll go back to the den and maybe between us we can find out what is wrong."

"Who's Anna?" Betty Lou asked as she helped clear the breakfast table.

"The lady who cleans for us every week. A really super person."

As Vickie passed her mother, perched on the padded kitchen counter stool, she could hear Anna's excited voice pouring out words at the other end of the line. She stopped to listen as her mother said quickly and firmly, "Of course we don't believe you would do something like that. Anna, I'm so sorry. I would never have recommended her to you if I had had any idea such a dreadful thing would happen to you."

Vickie caught her mother's attention and moved her

lips soundlessly. "What's the matter?"

But her mother shook her head and continued to listen to the excited sounds. Vickie could faintly hear her father's voice in the den as he talked on the extension. Then Mrs. Montgomery said, "We will do everything we can to help you. Try not to worry."

Mrs. Montgomery hung back the wall phone and stopped long enough to say, "Francine, will you help Vickie and Betty Lou get out all the silver and make sure nothing needs polishing? I think Anna did it all on Tuesday. But I had asked her to do so much that day, she might not have had time for it all, especially since Vickie wasn't home to help her. I'll be back in a moment."

She hurried along the hall, and the girls heard the door of the den close behind her.

"It sounds as though Anna is in serious trouble." Francine's voice was as worried-sounding as Vickie felt. "I wonder what it is."

"They'll probably tell you but not me," Vickie answered, her voice grumpy. "They always think I'm too young to know things."

"Sometimes it's better not to know about the problems, if you can't do anything about them," Francine answered. Then she added, "But if this concerns Anna personally, then I think they will tell you. She's important to all of us."

Vickie started to load the dishwasher and then heard her father call, "Vickie, could you come here a minute, please?"

Francine grinned impishly at her. "So it's you they are going to tell this time. Now don't you forget me. Remember, *I'm* not a child any longer."

Vickie wrinkled her nose and went into the den.

Her father's face and voice were serious as he asked,

"Has Diane said anything to you about jewelry missing from their apartment?"

"Uh-huh."

"When did she tell you?"

"Yesterday, I think. Yeah, she called me yesterday."

"Did she tell you just when they missed it?"

Vickie thought back, remembering the dreadful picture of Mrs. Stewart swaying in the lobby, her voice saying loud, swearing things to Charlie, and said, "Well, night before last when Betty Lou and I were over there, Mrs. Stewart wasn't home. She was at a party."

Vickie stopped and then went on, "When Diane called the next morning, she said her mother had looked for the bracelets when she got home from the party and couldn't find them. Is that what Anna called about? Is Mrs. Stewart blaming her?" she asked in sudden alarm.

Mrs. Montgomery nodded. Her voice was heavy with regret as she replied, "Poor Anna. She hasn't a dishonest bone in her body, and to be accused of stealing is such an insult to her. If I had not bragged so much to Mrs. Stewart about Anna, she wouldn't be in this trouble."

"Does Anna know exactly what is missing?"

Her mother gave a faint smile. "She just said 'joolry'."

"Diane told me they were heavy, gold, antique bracelets. I guess they have been in the family for a couple of generations. Some famous person gave them to someone in the family a long time ago. Diane said her grandmother thinks they are the most important thing they own."

"And Diane said her mother looked for them that night after she came home from the party?" Mr. Montgomery questioned.

Vickie nodded.

"Had she worn them when she went out?"

Vickie shrugged. "I don't know. But what difference

would—" Then the meaning of the question caught at her. "You mean maybe she lost them before she got home and didn't remember that she had worn them?"

She thought about the question. That was possible, of course, considering what Mrs. Stewart was like when she came home. Either she had lost them and did not notice it or had put them away and forgotten where. But they could not say that to Diane and reveal they knew about her mother's drinking problem.

When she did not answer, her father asked, "Were you girls still there when Diane's mother came home?"

"Not—not in the apartment, no," Vickie answered cautiously.

Her father's look was sharp, questioning. But he did not demand an explanation for her slow, hesitant answer, as he sat drumming his fingers on the desk top. His forehead knotted over the problem.

Then Vickie said suddenly, "When Diane called yesterday, she said she had been hunting that morning, which was Friday. So if the bracelets were lost—or taken—Wednesday or Thursday, that would let Anna out since she cleans there always on Tuesday."

Vickie stopped as her father shook his head. "But we do not know when Mrs. Stewart last saw them. She's not clear on that herself." He frowned and shook his head again. "I find it hard to believe that they were stolen by an outsider. Who could get into the apartment—"

"Perhaps she didn't lock the door some time," Mrs. Montgomery interrupted.

"She told me in no uncertain tones that she always locks the door and has trained Diane always to do so. I suppose that's why she has pounced on Anna as the guilty person."

Her thoughts a jumble of dismay, Vickie burst out,

47

"But Anna just wouldn't steal. She never would!"

"*We* know that," her father agreed. "But we must have proof. Anna has asked me to help, and of course I shall do all I can."

Shaking his head, he threw out his hands in a futile gesture. "Mrs. Stewart has apparently made up her mind that Anna is the thief and is threatening to have her arrested if she doesn't return the bracelets today. I promised Anna I would call Mrs. Stewart and ask her not to take action until Monday at least."

"Poor Anna," Mrs. Montgomery said softly. "How sad to have Christmas spoiled for her in this way."

"Does Diane know her mother is blaming Anna?" Vickie asked.

"I suppose she must. Mrs. Stewart apparently was very angry when she called Anna."

"It will be awkward to know what to say to her when she and Diane come for the open house this evening." Mrs. Montgomery frowned over the problem.

Her husband reached for the phone. "I had better call Mrs. Stewart and speak for Anna. A situation like this that involves people one knows is always difficult to handle."

Mrs. Montgomery stood up and looked sympathetically at Vickie. "You must try to put it out of your mind while we see what develops. Probably the less you and Diane talk about it, the better it will be—especially if Diane agrees with her mother."

Her father nodded. "Yes, we would not have mentioned it to you now except that you heard Anna's agitated voice. Then too, I thought Diane might have said something to you that would give a clue as to where the jewelry might be. I still think Mrs. Stewart put it away for safekeeping and forgot about it. We all do things like that occasionally.

The problem will be to convince her—tactfully."

The riddle went with Vickie the rest of the day. It filled her thoughts as she arranged bowls of holly on the polished end tables, inserted slim tapers in the candleholders on the buffet table, folded the delicate Christmas napkins, and placed cookies on the silver trays.

She worried most about Mrs. Stewart coming to the open house and hoped a lot of people would be there so there would not be time to talk. What if Diane also thought Anna was guilty?

"I'll stick up for Anna, no matter what," she told herself firmly.

People began to arrive just as the lights went on in the courtyard, making the decorations on the outdoor trees look like sparkling jewels. Mrs. Montgomery had asked Betty Lou to show guests where to put their coats so that she would be able to visit with everyone she knew and answer questions about her father.

"After all, this year's open house is as much for Betty Lou's benefit as for ours," she reminded them.

She had sent invitations, staggering the hours so that not everyone would come at the same time. Even so, the apartment overflowed with people. Lots of those who came early found it hard to leave. They kept exclaiming over the beauty of the spacious apartment and stood at the windows to look out over the glittering city lights that reflected on the still clean layer of snow that had fallen softly all afternoon.

Vickie and Betty Lou opened the door to two families who came together. Susie, the four-year-old, carried a little kitten, a Christmas present she could not bear to leave at home. Its tiny nose, a white star at the tip, peeked out from the blanket wrapped around it.

As Betty Lou turned away with Susie and the kitten,

Vickie answered the door chime again and opened the door to Diane and her mother.

"We are on our way to the airport to meet my mother's plane," Mrs. Stewart said to Mrs. Montgomery who came up behind Vickie. "We can only stay a minute or two. But I couldn't resist coming to see how you handle a large open house on Christmas Eve. You must have entertaining secrets that I don't know about."

Vickie did not hear her mother's answer. She was too busy worrying about the awful thought that struck her. Even though this smiling, gracious, impeccably dressed woman did not resemble the unkempt, rough-sounding one down in the apartment lobby, she *was* the same person. The minute Betty Lou saw her, she would recognize her. Somehow at that moment it seemed terribly important that Betty Lou not know that drunk woman was Diane's mother.

She looked around frantically, not even speaking to Diane who was slipping out of her coat. Betty Lou had gone into her bedroom with Susie and the kitten. Vickie hurried after them, her words spilling out.

"Betty Lou, can you help? Do you mind staying here and keeping Susie and the kitten with you for a few minutes? We've got—" She stopped and then started again. "Some people just came who—"

Her mind searched for some reason that Betty Lou would accept without thinking something was up. "We've got some people here who are allergic to cats. And kittens," she added hastily. "They're not going to stay long so keep the kitten here. OK?"

She listened to Betty Lou's, "Don't worry. It won't get out." But all the time her mind said, "That's another lie."

Whenever you got into any kind of mysterious business or had to keep a secret from someone, it seemed you always ended up telling lies. It had been that way last summer when she had tried to figure out the signals from Diane's apartment.

But this was no time to worry about lying. And anyway, *somebody* was probably allergic to cats. Now her main problem was to keep Betty Lou and Mrs. Stewart apart. She slipped out of the bedroom and closed the door behind her.

5

Vickie stood with her back against the closed door, feeling like a guard on sentry duty or a school hall monitor. She hoped her mother would not notice. Closed doors did not belong at the kind of open house her mother believed in. But this was only for the little while that Mrs. Stewart would stay.

She stretched to see around people, hunting for Mrs. Stewart, but could not see her with any of the groups of people in the living room. Vickie turned toward the dining room. Her job was to refill cookie plates so she had better check on them. Maybe on the way she would spot Mrs. Stewart. She had taken only a couple of steps when her father stopped her.

"You have a problem?" His voice was quiet and the question was really a statement.

Vickie nodded. "But—I—I don't know how to explain—"

He interrupted. "You don't want Mrs. Stewart to see Betty Lou. Or is it the other way around?" His eyes studied her face.

"How did you know?"

He patted her arm reassuringly. "Don't worry. I do not believe anyone else noticed. But I was close enough to see the connection between Mrs. Stewart's arrival and the quick way you shut Betty Lou into the bedroom. I am sure you have a good reason, so let me help keep Mrs. Stewart occupied."

Vickie watched him cross the room, talking to people on the way, nodding at everyone who spoke to him and laughing at their remarks. He reached Mrs. Stewart, standing just beyond the piano. Vickie watched him begin a conversation with her.

"Where's your friend?"

She jumped at the words spoken suddenly behind her and turned to look at Diane. She wondered, uneasily, how long Diane had been standing so near. Had she overheard the conversation with her father? Or watched, as Vickie had, his singleminded course across the room to Mrs. Stewart? She could not tell from the expression on Diane's face.

Diane stood with her hands clasped behind her. Vickie felt a rush of affection for her. No one would suspect that she wore a body cast under her red turtleneck cashmere sweater and gray flared jumper. Her determination to be normal and not let anyone know she had scoliosis made her walk with a light, springy step even though her back often hurt.

"Where's your friend?" Diane asked again.

"Susie brought the cutest little kitten with her, and she and Betty Lou have it in the bedroom. Want to see it?"

"Sure."

Vickie opened the door just wide enough for them to slide in and closed it quickly behind her.

"I don't want the kitten to get out," she answered Diane's questioning look. "It's so tiny, it could get stepped on by the mob of people out there."

Betty Lou was sitting with Susie on the floor between the twin beds. She was holding up a ribbon and they were laughing as the kitten reached out first one unsteady paw and then the other to swipe at it.

"It's darling!" Diane dropped down awkwardly on the

floor and reached to lift the ball of soft gray fur onto her lap. She looked at Susie. "What's her name?"

Susie stuck her finger in her mouth and ducked her head away. Then she shyly smiled back. "Misty," she said, her voice a whisper.

Diane went on talking softly to her, stroking the kitten's soft fur. Vickie watched Diane sitting completely absorbed in Susie and the kitten, and saw again the charm Diane had to draw people to her. But a troubling, disloyal thought forced its way into her mind. She was discovering that Diane could just as easily turn off the charm, and freeze out someone she decided she did not like. She was doing that now to Betty Lou, completely ignoring her as though she were not sitting there twelve inches away.

"She looks almost exactly like my kitten," Betty Lou said, "except that mine has a white place under the chin." She looked around and up at Vickie. "I wanted to give you one from the last litter, but my mother said you can't have pets in the apartment."

"That's silly." Diane's voice showed her scorn. "You don't have to tell anyone that you've got a pet. My mother says that what the management office doesn't know, they can't object to. *I* would have a pet except my mother can't stand animals."

There it was again. It was the one thing about Diane that had troubled her ever since they had met. She obeyed rules if she felt like it and broke them if she thought they were silly or unnecessary. Sometimes she envied Diane's freedom from rules like those her parents set for her and expected her to obey. Diane's mother just shrugged off rules she thought were unimportant. Of course, that was why Diane did too, so it was not really her fault that she was that way.

Vickie looked down uncertainly at Diane. She and

Susie played with the kitten, while Betty Lou, shoved aside by both of them, leaned against the bed, her back to the door, hugging her knees. And Vickie wondered. Maybe she was silly just to do what her folks said without thinking whether she had a right not to. She struggled with the thought, wondering if she were missing out on something by not being independent the way Diane was. After all, everyone liked Diane. That is, everyone she let like her.

Her thoughts were interrupted as the door opened. She looked around at Mrs. Stewart framed in the open bedroom doorway. Vickie darted an anxious look at Betty Lou, relieved that she was so absorbed in the kitten's antics that she did not look around.

Mrs. Stewart smiled at Vickie. "Your parents really know how to throw a party. Sorry we can't stay longer to enjoy it. Come, Diane. You know your grandmother is impatient at tardiness."

Without waiting for an answer, she turned and walked along the wide hall to the front door, standing for a moment under the mistletoe that swung gently from the hall chandelier. Vickie followed and watched her father help Mrs. Stewart with her coat and saw the way she smiled up at him. Something about the smile and the way she leaned toward him made Vickie feel uncomfortable. Then he said something to her, and she saw Mrs. Stewart clip off her smile.

She stiffened and shook her head. Vickie heard her low, husky voice as she replied, "She has already spoiled *my* Christmas, so why should I be considerate of hers? That's the trouble with our so-called justice these days. The victim's rights are always ignored in favor of the criminal's."

She pulled her mink coat closer around her shoulders

and lifted her chin, her lips a thin line and her eyes narrowed in anger. Then she shrugged. "Oh, all right. I won't press charges against her until Tuesday. There's one thing she must keep in mind, however. Even if she returns the bracelets, she needn't expect to work for me any longer. I won't have a thief in my house."

Vickie heard a sharp intake of breath behind her. She turned to see Diane, motionless, with one arm in the sleeve of her coat, the rest dragging on the floor. The strange, shocked expression on her face puzzled Vickie. Diane looked as though something heavy had suddenly hit her. Vickie was sure she saw total surprise and dismay wash over Diane's face as she stared at her mother, still looking defiantly at Mr. Montgomery.

Vickie looked from her to Mrs. Stewart. What had there been in her mother's words that had taken Diane so completely by surprise? Diane knew the bracelets were gone; she certainly must know that her mother intended to go to the police about it. And she certainly should know that her mother would not forgive Anna and let her work for them any longer. That was all Mrs. Stewart had said. Why would Diane be so completely floored by that?

It must be because she liked Anna so much. When she had first met Anna last summer, she had laughed at her "funny way of talking." She had thought Vickie was silly to help with her cleaning jobs and said, "That's what she's getting paid for. I wouldn't let her boss me around the way she does you."

But when Mrs. Montgomery had recommended Anna to Mrs. Stewart, and Anna had agreed to clean there Tuesday mornings, Diane had gradually changed her mind about her.

"The thing about her is that she really *listens* to you," Diane said once to Vickie.

Now Vickie watched Diane struggle into her coat, carefully avoid looking at anyone, mumble her thanks, and follow her mother out the door. She wondered if her father had noticed Diane's face. He was used to figuring out what people's reactions and expressions meant.

But when she asked him later as they helped straighten the furniture and clear the dishes after everyone had left, he shook his head slowly.

"No, I wasn't looking at Diane just then." He stood chewing at his lip and frowning into space. Then he said, "If Mrs. Stewart presses charges against Anna as she is determined to do, it will be very difficult for Anna. Mrs. Stewart has made up her mind that Anna is guilty—"

"But she's *not*!"

"I agree with my heart, but my mind says we must *prove* her innocence. In the meantime we must think of Anna's pride and of her reputation. If word of this gets around, other women for whom she cleans might be suspicious of her even though they have no cause to."

"That means we have to find who did take the bracelets."

"That's the puzzle we have to solve," her father agreed. "Mrs. Stewart says nothing else is missing. She insists that only Anna has been in the apartment—aside, of course, from herself and Diane. Someone could possibly have come in and left no evidence of a break-in. But why would that someone have gone directly to where the bracelets were kept and taken them and nothing else? Undoubtedly Mrs. Stewart has other jewelry."

Vickie nodded. "And I think some of it is pretty expensive, stuff she got when she was married. But the bracelets are what she really likes."

Vickie watched her father stand, his eyes thoughtful.

She could practically see his legal mind turning over every piece of the puzzle.

He said slowly, "I have suggested to Mrs. Stewart that she simply mislaid them. She insists not. Was quite angry about it, in fact." His smile was rueful as he looked at Vickie before he went on. "Apparently Diane is just as positive that they have been stolen. She says she is sure they were in their usual place in the jewelry case when her mother got out some pieces earlier in the week."

Thinking back, Vickie wrinkled her forehead. "I'm all mixed up, because Mrs. Stewart was out a lot last week. The time Betty Lou and I went over, Thursday, she hadn't been home after work. She had stayed for a party."

She could not help remembering the dreadful picture of Mrs. Stewart swaying in the lobby, her voice saying ugly things. She stopped abruptly. She felt her father's sharp, questioning glance, but instead of asking any questions, he only said, "I see," his voice thoughtful.

Then Vickie burst out. "I still say that all we have to do is to discover when Mrs. Stewart last saw the bracelets. If they were still there Thursday or Wednesday, then Anna can't be blamed since she cleans there always on Tuesdays."

Mr. Montgomery laughed as he looked at her. "That's the second time you've come up with that sharp bit of detective work. I'm going to have to change the name of the law firm to read 'Montgomery and Daughter'."

In spite of his laugh, Vickie detected an unexpectedly serious note in his voice. "Vickie, could you talk to Diane on Monday? Alone, without Betty Lou around? I'm anxious to keep the investigation very quiet in order not to hurt Anna any more than she has been already simply by Mrs. Stewart's suspicions of her. To be called a thief is a terrible indignity to her."

"But what do you want me to talk to Diane about?"

"Just ask her for more information. Try to find out why she is so positive Anna isn't guilty—"

"Well, *we're* just as positive."

"I know, but we're on the outside of the case; Diane is right in the middle of it. She might know facts she—well—hasn't thought of, has not mentioned. Ask her if she has any idea who else could have taken them."

"Yeah, but Diane might—might—"

"Tell you it's none of your business?" he finished for her.

When she nodded, he said slowly, "But perhaps in the long run you might be helping Diane if you give her a chance to talk about it just to you. She might tell you facts that she wouldn't tell anyone else. I would judge that you are her best friend."

His voice ended on a questioning note, and Vickie said, "Yes," adding quickly, "And she is my best friend."

"Well, remember, best friends remain best friends no matter what." He gave her a quick hug as he went to help close the big dining-room table.

Vickie looked after him, puzzled. She was trying to sort out the questions crowding her mind. He must know something she did not. Maybe he thought Mrs. Stewart had purposely lost the bracelets. She remembered her father talking about cases where people reported things missing just to collect insurance on them. She thought about Mrs. Stewart. Would she do something like that? Maybe. And would Diane know about it? Could that be why she was so shocked to hear her mother blame Anna?

She helped straighten the living room, turning the problem over in her mind as she listened to Betty Lou running on about the people she had talked to.

When her father, yawning, turned out the living room lamps and the tree lights, he said, "Don't forget, everyone.

Set your alarms early enough to get up and open packages."

"Who needs an alarm for that?" Betty Lou asked.

"You—you still want us all to go to church?"

Vickie heard the shading of reluctance in her mother's voice and knew her father had too. He answered very seriously, looking back at her, his voice quiet. "Yes, I do want it—very much."

Vickie watched them stand looking at one another as though she and Francine and Betty Lou were not even there. They seemed to be carrying on a silent conversation, one they had started sometime earlier and had not quite finished. One on which they had widely different viewpoints, and yet they still respected the other's opinion.

Then her father said, his voice still carrying that quiet, determined note, "I don't know why this means so much to me, Louise. But it does. It is very important."

Her mother smiled then and said in her usual happy, lighthearted way, "Why, then, if it is important to you, it is important to all of us."

She looked around at them. "Remember, the last one up tomorrow is the last one to open his gifts."

6

Lilting notes from the piano woke Vickie in the early morning darkness, and she listened to her father's one-fingered rendition of "Jingle Bells." Every Christmas morning that she could remember, he had played that tune, and always before she had leaped out of bed and raced barefooted down the stairs. She had always hoped she would plop down in front of the enormous lighted tree before he finished the "jingle all the way" part, but she never quite made it.

Today she stayed curled under the soft warmth of the blanket, listening to the happy lilt of the tune as her father finished it and started over again. She heard Francine opening dresser drawers in her room. Then Betty Lou snapped upright and threw back the covers.

"Hey, Vickie! It's Christmas! Get up!"

Vickie grabbed her robe, thrust her feet into slippers, and followed Betty Lou into the den. Opening Christmas packages had always been a special time in their family. The mad scramble as children to see what they had gotten gradually gave way to an interest in what the rest of the family had received. Today was the same. Then Mrs. Montgomery began gathering up the drifts of silver and gold and green papers and ribbons.

"Save the ribbons and bows, girls. They are too pretty to throw away. Let's straighten the room before your father has breakfast ready."

Vickie could tell her father wanted to keep all their traditional family customs even though he had added this new feature of going to church. She heard him whistling in the kitchen where he was measuring coffee and scrambling eggs just as he had done every other Christmas morning. His specialty was a delicate, flaky, melt-in-your-mouth Christmas stollen he made himself, carrying on a tradition from his childhood as his father had done, and *his* father before that.

Francine helped herself to an unheard-of third piece of the stollen as she said, "Pete couldn't believe that the noted lawyer Carl Montgomery was also a baker, when I told him about this coffee cake. You have really impressed him as a super father as well as a super lawyer."

She propped her elbows on the table, coffee cup cradled in both hands, and looked affectionately at her father.

"I gather Pete had a lonely childhood," he answered. "Happy but lonely. He was never able to get close to his father. It was not entirely his father's fault, since as a military man he was away a good deal from the family. And apparently he had the idea that showing affection to a son was somewhat unmanly, might make him a sissy. Peter was in high school before he was sure that his father really loved him."

Vickie, listening, remembered what Pete had told her last summer about his being lonely and having to make friends fast because they moved around so much.

"How do you know so much about Pete?" Francine demanded.

"We have talked." Mr. Montgomery looked across at her, a twinkle in his eyes but seriousness in his voice as he went on. "If I am going to give someone one of my treasures, I insist on knowing if that someone is worthy of the gift."

Francine looked back at him, her face and voice equally serious, and answered, "Pete is."

Then she took a last quick swallow of coffee and said, "Pete is going to meet us at the church. He surprised me— he acted as though he really wants to go."

"That's because you're going," Vickie reminded her. "The way he acts, he'd follow you to—to—"

"Alaska?" her father suggested.

"Well, that's about where we are today from the way it looks outside," Francine retorted. "Excuse me while I go put on warm somethings or other."

"You should have grown up in Minnesota if you think this is cold," her father called after her.

Betty Lou went to dress too, but Vickie sat at the table, remembering last summer's talk with Pete, and what he had said about going to Sunday school and the Bible verses he had talked about. She wondered if Pete and her father talked about the Bible when they ate lunch together, and if Pete had ever told him about the Bible verse that reminded him of Francine.

Vickie drew her eyebrows together in a puzzled frown as she thought about her father. All her life she had thought he knew the answer to everything. And if he did not know an answer right off, he could reach for one of the many books that lined the walls of the den and flip to the right page. But now only the Bible seemed to have the answers he was looking for. When she went into the den at unexpected times in the evening, she found him sitting in his big, soft, leather chair, his Bible open in front of him, a questioning look on his face, while the stereo played symphonies as a soothing background. She remembered asking him once if the Bible was harder to understand than his thick law books. He had looked at her thoughtfully, giving his full attention to her question the way he always did.

Then he had said, "The words are easier to understand, but the thoughts are harder, because they are God's thoughts, not man's. At least—that's what the Bible claims."

She had frowned back at him. "What do you mean?"

"Well, take this story." He looked up a page number in the index and turned to it. "It's about a young boy who gave his lunch, just a small one, to Jesus. Jesus was able to make it feed five thousand people." He looked at her. "Those are easy words to understand, aren't they?"

"Yes, but how could He do that?"

"Well, you see, that is the part that is difficult to understand. But the Bible says Jesus did miracles because He was—is—God."

"I don't understand."

Her father's voice was groping as he answered, "I don't either. But I have to believe it."

"Why?"

"Because of the evidence. I can't get away from it. It rings so true."

The remembered conversation tumbled in her mind as she sat drinking her cup of cocoa, half listening to the comfortably relaxed conversation between her parents.

"This is only an experiment, Louise, not something permanent. I hope you understand that."

Vickie saw her mother nod quickly and reach to put her hand over his. "I know. Your lawyer mind simply has to follow an idea through until you are completely satisfied as to whether or not it is true. I only hope—" She stopped, biting her lip.

"What? That I won't decide to make it permanent?"

"No, no," she answered quickly. "My main concern is

that you not be disappointed."

Vickie's train of thought exploded in a question. "Did you know that Pete knows about John 3:16?"

She saw her mother's questioning look and her father's quick nod as he answered, "Yes. But he didn't say he had talked to you about it."

How nice Pete was. Vickie was swept again by liking for him. He had not blabbed about their talk last summer. Instead, he had treated her like a grownup and had kept their talk confidential.

She stood up and picked up her dishes. "Well, we had a private talk once about serious things."

As she went into the kitchen she heard her mother ask in a bewildered tone, *"What* is John 3:16?"

She waited to hear her father answer. "Why, it is really the Christmas story, Louise. It is Vickie's manger scene. For God so loved the world that He gave His Son."

Vickie went into the bedroom. Betty Lou looked around. "It sure seems funny to be going to church on Christmas instead of watching games on TV or doing something fun. Remember when we were little—how we ran back and forth to each other's house and spent all Christmas day playing with our new stuff?" She finished smoothing the bedspread and asked, "Is Diane going with us?"

Vickie shook her head. "No." She had not wanted to tell Diane they were going to church, afraid she would laugh.

When she came out of the shower, she saw Betty Lou looking out the window. Without turning around Betty Lou asked, "What's Diane's father like?"

"I don't know," Vickie answered quickly. Then she added, "Her parents are divorced."

"Oh, I didn't know that. I thought maybe he was—he

was—dead." Betty Lou forced out the word, and Vickie shot her a quick glance, understanding why she did not want even to say the word. Her father had come so close to dying this week that even the thought was scary to her.

"I guess not having a father bothers Diane, even though she doesn't talk about it," Vickie said slowly. She wished she knew how to explain one best friend to another best friend. "She pretends she doesn't care that her father just walked out and left her and her mother. But I'm sure it must bother her."

"Maybe she doesn't care," Betty Lou answered. "Feelings don't seem to bother her. Other people's feelings anyway." Her usually sympathetic, understanding voice was hard.

There was not time to explain or to defend Diane because it was time to go, and they heard Mrs. Montgomery call, "Girls, are you ready?"

"We may have to wait a few minutes for a taxi," Mr. Montgomery said as they rode down in the elevator. "The drivers won't be expecting many people to be out on a Christmas Sunday morning, so they won't be cruising around looking for fares."

But when they reached the lobby, Mac swung his heavy cape around his shoulders and went out with a whistle to flag a cab. They crowded in, and Mr. Montgomery gave the address of a church on the boulevard. It was a short ride on the snowy streets and quick, because there was very little traffic. The driver pulled to a stop in front of a beautiful building. Winter-browned ivy clung to the gray brick. The building sat well back from the wide avenue, and the surrounding grounds were blanketed with deep glistening snowdrifts.

Organ music swept them in through the wide double doors and walked them down the carpeted aisle behind a man in a dark suit with a white rose in his lapel. The church was quite full, but an almost vacant row about halfway down the aisle had room for them all. Francine and Pete went into the row first, then Betty Lou and Vickie. But people were being shown in on the other end, taking the rest of the space. Their usher murmured apologies and put Mr. and Mrs. Montgomery in the row just ahead.

Vickie watched the choir come in wearing dark green robes and followed by the minister, who smiled in a friendly way as he looked out at the congregation. Everything was so unfamiliar that Vickie kept checking the paper the usher had handed them, giving the outline of the service.

The minister announced that since this was a special Christmas service, the choir would present a miniature concert of specially selected Christmas songs that would appeal to everyone. Then he would close with a brief meditation. He smiled around at them as he added, "I mustn't keep you children too long from your new toys and you parents from your turkey."

Vickie was glad he was not going to do a lot of talking. The music she could enjoy, but a long talk would be boring.

They all joined in singing "Away in a Manger," a song she remembered from grade school Christmas programs. Other numbers the choir sang she had heard on television or had heard on downtown street corners by Salvation Army people ringing bells and blaring the melody on brass instruments. Vickie knew her mother seldom passed one of the bell ringers without dropping money into the kettle.

The choir sang "Deck the Halls," and she and Betty Lou nudged each other. They had to hold back giggles, remembering last year's school play. A couple of boys had written silly words to the music and sung them and made the teacher angry. Then the choir sang "I'm Dreaming of a White Christmas," one of her mother's favorites.

"It reeks of sentiment," she always said, "but I like it anyway."

When the minister finally stood up to speak, his comfortable voice and very relaxed manner made it easy to listen to him. For some reason, Vickie had expected he would talk loud and long. He was interesting. He told a lot of stories about Christmas in his family and the funny things his children said and did.

She could tell from the way her father sat that he was listening intently. His concentrated interest showed in the way he held his head and shoulders, leaning forward slightly and sitting motionless, his eyes looking straight up at the minister. Vickie was so busy watching him and thinking what a good-looking, neat father he was, that she only half listened to the minister talk.

But as she watched her father, she saw him shift slightly and lean back, his attention becoming less intent. Then he reached into his inner coat pocket, fumbling for something. When he pulled his hand out, Vickie sat up straighter and leaned forward a little, stretching her neck to see what he had in his hand.

She could not tell at first, because he held his hand close to him and slightly to one side. It made her more curious and she leaned farther forward. She saw then that he held a small, leather book. At first she thought it was the little pocket appointment book he always carried. But as he lifted it slightly and turned a page, she could see that it had printing and not the lines and dates of an appointment book. It was not a Bible, because it was too small. Unless it was just part of the Bible. A few chapters maybe?

The rustle of the audience let her know that the service was over. She stood with the rest of the family for a closing song and waited for the minister's brief prayer.

Quite a few people spoke to her parents as they moved slowly along the crowded aisle on the way to the door. She saw her father's startled look at one man who pumped Mr. Montgomery's hand enthusiastically and urged him to come regularly.

"Great church, this," he boomed. "I've been a member here for twenty-five years."

She heard her mother's low, "Isn't that the man who was arrested for—?" and saw her father's quick nod at the unfinished question.

A couple of young girls stood at the end of one row, whispering to each other as they looked at Francine.

"Are you a movie star?" one of them asked.

Francine laughed and shook her head.

"I've seen you somewhere," the girl insisted. "I bet I've seen your picture on a magazine someplace."

Francine shook her head again, and Pete took her arm and hurried her along. They followed Mr. Montgomery who went out a different entrance from where the minister was standing shaking hands with people.

They piled into the taxi Mr. Montgomery waved down. Vickie and Betty Lou sat on the edge of the seat so there would be room for them all.

"I'm only supposed to take four passengers," the driver said. "But you gals are so little, you won't even be noticed."

No one talked on the quick ride home. Vickie could tell from the way her father stared out at the quiet streets that something bothered him. When they reached the apartment and hung their coats away, Mrs. Montgomery stopped them all in the hall.

"Before we do anything about dinner, I think we should thank your father for taking us to church this morning. It was a lovely thing to do on Christmas morning, and I feel quite refreshed."

But Mr. Montgomery shook his head and turned to walk slowly into the den. He looked around at them as they followed him. "I'm not sure it was a good idea after all," he answered. His voice was groping. He reached to aimlessly shift a paperweight on the desk a few inches one way and then back again. Vickie could tell how deeply he felt, because he was hunting for words that usually came so readily to his lips.

"I thought on Christmas at church we would hear about—about royalty—about majesty, even though Christmas commemorates just the birth of a baby."

His hands moved helplessly as he tried to explain. "Instead, we heard the kind of music we hear on a TV variety show and were told cute sayings of children and sentimental stories about going home for Christmas."

He picked up the Bible lying on the desk, holding it tightly in both hands. "When I read the story in here, it didn't sound so ordinary, so commonplace. That's why I wanted to know more about it."

He opened the Bible. "The story is in one of the books in the back," he said, fumbling through the thin pages. "Here it is."

He stood looking down at the words. Then Vickie heard her mother's light voice. "Read it to us please, Carl."

He looked at her gratefully. "It's in the second chapter of the book called Luke. I've discovered that a lot of the Bible books are named for the men who wrote them," he explained.

He began, his voice unsteady at first, but growing

strong and sure as he read.

And it came to pass in those days, that there went out a decree from Caesar Augustus, that all the world should be taxed. (And this taxing was first made when Cyrenius was governor of Syria.) And all went to be taxed, every one into his own city. And Joseph also went up from Galilee, out of the city of Nazareth, into Judea, unto the city of David, which is called Bethlehem; (because he was of the house and lineage of David:) to be taxed with Mary his espoused wife, being great with child. And so it was, that, while they were there, the days were accomplished that she should be delivered. And she brought forth her first-born son, and wrapped him in swaddling clothes, and laid him in a manger; because there was no room for them in the inn. And there were in the same country shepherds abiding in the field, keeping watch over their flock by night. And, lo, the angel of the Lord came upon them, and the glory of the Lord shone round about them: and they were sore afraid. And the angel said unto them, Fear not: for, behold, I bring you good tidings of great joy, which shall be to all people. For unto you is born this day in the city of David a Saviour, which is Christ the Lord. And this shall be a sign unto you; Ye shall find the babe wrapped in swaddling clothes, lying in a manger. And suddenly there was with the angel a multitude of the heavenly host praising God, and saying, Glory to God in the highest, and on earth peace, good will toward men. And it came to pass, as the angels were gone away from them into heaven, the shepherds said one to another, Let us now go even unto Bethlehem, and see this thing which is come to pass, which the Lord hath made known

> unto us. And they came with haste, and found Mary,
> and Joseph, and the babe lying in a manger.

Vickie found herself blinking back tears as his quiet voice read the simple words. It was an exact description of her manger scene. She had not known it was pictured in the Bible so beautifully.

When he finished and closed the Bible, looking down at it, the room was still. Vickie looked around at Betty Lou half-hidden by Francine who was standing close to Pete. He was leaning against the wall by the door. His hands were in his pockets, and an intent look was on his face as he watched Mr. Montgomery. His lips were pursed in a soundless whistle.

She looked at her mother, standing behind the big desk chair. Her hands gripped the chair back so tightly that her knuckles showed white. They were all like statues, held motionless by the impact of the beautiful words.

Then Pete's voice, hushed, said, "If the minister had stood up and just read those words, that's all we would have needed."

Her father looked across at Pete, surprise in his eyes. "Exactly." Then he looked around at them and put the Bible down carefully. "I'm sorry I wasted your time this morning."

Her mother moved then from behind the chair and walked over to link her arm in his and look up at him with a smile.

"You didn't waste our time," she said. "We gave it to you. And maybe someplace there's a church, a minister, who will give you what you are looking for. Let's try again."

Vickie saw the gladness springing into his face as he looked down at her. "Thanks," he said softly.

He put his arm around her shoulders and smiled around at them. "Now let's go eat that turkey."

7

Vickie lifted her head in the darkened room and peered over at Betty Lou curled in the middle of the other bed. The blanket under which Betty Lou huddled was rising and falling with her soft breathing. Typical Betty Lou. She had always been the one at camp who had to be dragged out of bed in the morning, and even at slumber parties she collapsed before anyone else thought of sleep.

But this was vacation. Who wanted to stay in bed on vacation? Vickie slid out from under the warm blankets and felt for her slippers. If she could sneak into the bathroom and dress, she could get out and call Diane and get something fun planned for the day. And she needed a chance to follow Dad's suggestions and find out more about the missing bracelets. He must have some reason why he thought Betty Lou should be kept out of any talk about them. One thing they had to find out for sure was the time Mrs. Stewart first knew they were gone. The timing was crucial to Anna's being proved innocent.

Betty Lou turned over, pulling the blankets higher, but did not wake up as Vickie slipped out of the room and gently closed the door. Following the hum of voices, she found her parents in the den sitting on the couch in front of the fire having coffee. They were deep in conversation. Her father was holding the Bible open in one hand; his other arm was around Mrs. Montgomery's shoulders.

They looked around at her with a welcoming smile, and

her father said, "Come join us."

"How come you're home, Dad?"

"I decided to take the day off. Not too many people are thinking of lawyers the day after Christmas—"

"Except Mrs. Stewart." His wife's voice was sober as she interrupted.

"Even she has agreed to wait until Tuesday. I'm hoping we will have a solution by then."

Vickie turned toward the door. "I'm going to get something to eat. Then I want to call Diane before Betty Lou gets up."

Laughter colored her mother's voice as she said, "Unless Betty Lou has changed drastically, she is settled for the rest of the morning. I always envied Thelma her child's ability to sleep, since neither you nor Francine were that way. I didn't mind your being awake early; it was your being *up* that was the problem."

Vickie smiled back at her. "Well, we got that from somebody, didn't we?"

She went to the kitchen and got out milk and a pan to fix cocoa. While the milk heated, she poured a glass of orange juice and walked in to stand at the plant-filled windows at the end of the dining room. She sipped the juice and looked across the courtyard at the even white shades in Diane's apartment.

At almost nine in the morning, Diane was certainly awake, sitting up in bed, gulping a book. She always had a stack of books around that she was just beginning, was halfway through, or had just finished. Sometimes she had three or four going at the same time.

"Don't you get mixed up about who does what in which book?" Vickie remembered asking once.

"Of course not," Diane had answered, surprise in her voice. "They're all different people doing different things."

Vickie knew Diane got a lot of her interesting and sometimes crazy ideas from what she read in books. Like the idea of putting SOS and HELP signs in her window last summer to attract Vickie's attention instead of doing something so ordinary as calling directory assistance to get her phone number.

A smile tilted Vickie's mouth as she thought of the bold, black HELP signs Diane still plastered in the window to send over a message. Sometimes the sign meant *Help, I'm all alone; come on over.* Sometimes it meant *Help, I've got a whole chocolate cake to eat.* And other times, *Help, I don't have anyone to talk to.*

Vickie finished the orange juice, wondering for the hundredth time what made Diane so different from the friends she had had in grade school—Pam and Sandy and Betty Lou. Diane was fun to do things with, but they had been too. In fact, she had actually done more with them, swimming and bicycling and climbing trees in Betty Lou's back yard, things she could not do in the city and that Diane could not do at all because of her back trouble.

"I suppose I wouldn't do some of that stuff now if I still lived near them," she reminded herself, thinking about how growing up changed your idea of what was fun.

The thing with Diane was that she was always trying to help you be better than you were, even though she got impatient with you.

Vickie stared unseeing down into the courtyard. She remembered the first time she and Diane had bought a whole bunch of stuff downtown, going halves, and she had tried to figure out how much her share was.

"Good night, Vickie!" Diane had exclaimed. "It sure takes you a long time to add up a couple of numbers."

Vickie shrugged. "Oh, well, Francine says pretty soon they won't teach math in school anymore, because everyone will use computers."

"Yeah, but you still should know how to multiply in your head and add without counting on your fingers. Know what would help? Playing dominoes."

"Dominoes?" Vickie's voice had been doubtful.

"Sure. It's fun. And it'll teach you math."

So they had played endless games of dominoes all through August. It had been awful at first when she tried to add up the spots on the dominoes. Playing with the double-twelve set had been especially hard when there was a double twelve at one end and a double eleven or nine and maybe an eight at the other ends. And Diane had been merciless, pouncing on her and scolding every time she thought Vickie was counting on her fingers instead of adding the numbers in her head. But the games had paid off, and Vickie knew that even though she still did not like math, she had more confidence about working problems than she had ever had.

Diane had helped her with other subjects too. "Don't think of history as a dumb subject you've gotta learn. History is about people who do exciting things and live exciting lives."

"Yeah, that's what Dad and Francine keep telling me, but it doesn't sound that way in our social studies books."

"Look—what do you know about the French Revolution?"

"Nothing."

"Vickie!"

"Well—I mean, I've *heard* about it, but I don't remember much about dates and stuff."

"Boy, you sure must have gone to a dumb school. We studied about it in fifth grade."

"So?"

"So you oughta know about it by now in seventh."

76

Diane searched along a bookshelf and yanked out a book. "Here, read this story, and you'll never say history is a dumb subject."

Vickie took the book Diane thrust at her and read the title. *"A Tale of Two Cities?* OK."

A sizzling sound in the kitchen and the smell of burned chocolate made her dash to the kitchen and snatch the boiled-over pan of cocoa from the stove. Her mind was still on Diane, thinking of the many ways she had been a good friend.

And now Dad was suggesting that Diane needed her help. She was sure from the way he sounded that he meant help with more than just the bracelets. As she thought about the missing jewelry, a tiny frown pulled her eyebrows together. Diane was always impatient with people who did not catch on to things quickly. But her impatience never hurt the other person; it was always to help. That was what made her attitude toward Betty Lou so hard to understand.

"She hasn't really been one bit nice to Betty Lou." Vickie said the words out loud without meaning to, hating to admit the fact.

While she waited for the cocoa to cool enough to drink, she dialed Diane's number.

"Hi, what are you doing?"

"Reading."

Vickie laughed. "That figures. Want to do something today?"

"What?"

Vickie listened to the one-word answers, puzzled. In the six months she had known Diane, her voice had been happy and impatient and sad and discouraged and angry and indignant. But it had never had this closed-off sound that said so clearly Keep Out. She felt as though she were standing outside a high thick wall. Although she searched carefully all along its length, she could not find a door that would open to let her in. What was the matter with Diane anyway?

Then she heard Diane ask, "What do you want to do?"

"Well, you can come here or I can come over there."

"You don't need me. You've got Betty Lou."

So that *was* it. Diane was jealous of her friendship with Betty Lou and was just being sulky.

I should think she'd know a person can have more than one friend, she told herself indignantly. Aloud she said, "Betty Lou's still asleep. As soon as I finish breakfast, I'll come over."

She gulped the rest of the cocoa, closing her mind and eyes to a third slice of the Christmas bread and determining to lose five more pounds to go with the eight she had lost since summer.

When she pushed through the revolving doors in Diane's building, Charlie lifted his hand in a wave.

"Beats me how come you gals haven't figured some way to rig up a contraption between your two windows and hoist yourself back and forth. This way you sure have to ride up and down elevators a lot."

Vickie smiled back at him. "If we didn't come through the lobby past your desk, we'd never get to see your smiling face," she retorted.

As she answered, she realized this was another thing Diane had done for her. Last year she would just have smiled at Charlie and not been smart enough to think of a quick answer. She was not always sharp enough now, but at least she was better than she used to be.

When she got to Diane's apartment, she knocked their special signal, and Diane opened the door immediately.

Vickie followed her into her bedroom, still not sure how

soon she should turn the conversation around to the missing bracelets. Today Diane might not want to talk about them.

"Where did you go yesterday?" Diane asked as she plopped down on her bed. "I was looking out the window and saw you all walk across the courtyard. You were all dressed up and Mac got a taxi for you. I suppose you went to visit some more old friends." Her voice had a slightly bitter edge to it as she said the last sentence.

"We went to church," Vickie answered shortly.

"To church?" Diane repeated. Then she reddened. "Oh." Her voice sounded embarrassed and a little ashamed, and she looked away from Vickie. "I didn't call in the afternoon because I didn't think you were home. I thought—I just imagined you were having a good time visiting people."

"And I didn't call you when we got home, because your grandmother was here, and I thought you were busy doing things with her."

She tried not to let on she knew that Diane was jealous because she thought they were having fun with someone else and not including her. Not hurting the other person's feelings and being willing to be misunderstood was a part of friendship too.

To bridge the awkward moment, she asked, "What *did* you do yesterday?"

"Oh, opened presents after my mother and grandmother got up. They slept late. Then we went out for dinner to a hotel. Then we came home and sat around. And I read."

"How long is your grandmother staying?"

"She's gone. That's where my mother is now—taking her to the airport."

"Oh, I thought—I mean, since she came so far for Christmas—I just thought she would stay longer."

Diane shook her head, her lips twisted in a bitter smile. "She only comes for Christmas because she thinks it's a

79

family holiday and says families ought to be together that day. But she never stays. She never stayed when my fa—other years. If she stays too long, she and my mother fight." Diane gestured as though the subject were unimportant, but she looked away from the sympathy in Vickie's eyes.

Then she asked abruptly, "What loot did you get for Christmas?" Without waiting for an answer, she gestured around. "As usual I came out with a bunch of books. And clothes of course. And my grandmother gave me a year's subscription to *National Geographic* and *Seventeen*. My mother thinks the *National Geographic* thing is wild, but I like it. It's got pictures and descriptions of places I've never even heard of."

"Who knows? Maybe some day you'll be a world traveler."

"You know what I'd really like to be?" Eagerness lighted Diane's face, sparkling her eyes, as she sat in the middle of the bed. "I'd like to be an archaeologist."

"A what?"

"Archaeologist." Impatience surged in her voice as she explained, "You know. People who go around and explore in different countries where people used to live. They dig up places to see how people lived hundreds and hundreds of years ago."

Diane leaned forward, pouring out words. "It would be so neat! It would be like solving mysteries. You know, trying to figure out from looking at the dishes and pans you dig up what they ate and how they cooked their food. Did they wear shoes? Were they smart? Did the kids go to school and could they read? Did they have books even?"

"You never said you liked stuff like that."

Vickie watched the eagerness on Diane's face fade to a sullen frown. Her lips set in a thin straight line.

"Well, you don't know everything about me!" She

snapped out the words and stood up awkwardly. "You think that just because you've known me since summer I'm supposed to tell you everything I think and do."

"I do not!"

"You do too! All of a sudden you start arguing about every little thing I say."

"You're the one who started arguing." Vickie tried to keep her voice from sounding as angry as she felt. What was the matter with Diane anyway?

She watched Diane walk over to lean against the window frame. Her thin hands twisted the window shade cord. Seeing her narrow shoulders and the slim line of her figure, Vickie envied again Diane's being able to eat double hamburgers and two orders of french fries and a milk shake and never have any bulges.

It's funny, she thought, *how your mind can go along on different levels, thinking about two different things at the same time.* Here she stood thinking about her battle to lose weight and remembering the picture Pete had shown her that hot July day. It was a picture of Francine when she was almost thirteen, and fat. Pete had said, "If Francine can do it, you can."

The other part of her mind was saying, "How can I find out what's bugging Diane and help her?"

Then Diane half turned. Her voice was low and muffled as she said, "I'm sorry, Vickie. I didn't mean to blow up at you. It's just that—just that—"

She turned abruptly back to stare out the window and finished, "Everything is such a mess." She gestured with one hand. "Christmas is terrible. It always has been and especially the last couple of years. And then yesterday my mother and grandmother argued all day about my—about my—"

She looked around at Vickie and then away. Her voice

was a whisper, low and broken. "You don't know what it's like. Your father is home. He always does stuff with you, cares about you. Mine—" She stopped and swallowed.

After a minute she went on, "You're always talking about how many books I've read. I *had* to start reading when I was real little. It was the only way I could shut out the sound of my mother and father fighting. I had to find another world that I could escape to."

Vickie's throat was tight with a lump of pity as she listened. How could she have thought that Diane did not care about her father, did not care that her parents were divorced, when actually it hurt so much that she *couldn't* talk about it.

But as she took an involuntary step toward her, Diane's figure stiffened and she turned to face Vickie. As though regretting the glimpse she had given of herself, she said, her voice angry, "And now there's this thing with Anna."

Vickie hesitated, wanting someway to show Diane that she understood and felt sorry for her. But Diane was making clear that she did not want any pity. So she said, "Yeah, what are we going to do? I don't think she took the bracelets, as I've said a hundred times."

"I don't either, but my mother is positive."

"Anna called and asked my father to help her."

Diane went on as though she had not heard, as though she were endlessly arguing something in her mind. "I didn't know that my mother would blame Anna. I asked her why, and she said cleaning women always looked for stuff they could steal. And then she said who else could it be? And I don't know what to do about it, how to change her mind."

"Well, that is the question," Vickie answered. "I mean, who did take them? It has to be either Anna or a burglar. But if it was a burglar, how come nothing else is missing?

A burglar would have taken other things, wouldn't he?"

"Maybe my mother just hasn't missed anything else yet," Diane answered, her eyes looking past Vickie.

"It's kind of scary to think of burglars in this building when it has such tight security. How could someone get past Charlie?"

"I don't think anyone could," Diane answered. "That's why I think it was someone in the building—"

"You mean, one of your neighbors?"

Diane shrugged. "Well, someone who was let in by someone else—a friend."

Vickie was not sure just what Diane meant. After a moment, she asked, "Are you sure your mother didn't just put the bracelets somewhere different and forget about where?"

"No!" Diane's voice was so explosively angry that Vickie stared at her.

Diane gestured in apology. "I'm sorry. I shouldn't get mad at you. But I'm worried. My mother is so positive Anna is guilty that I don't see how even your father can help her. Somehow *we've* got to prove she isn't guilty. And the only way to do that is to find the bracelets."

8

Vickie nodded. "OK, I agree. But how are we going to find a couple of solid gold bracelets that have just disappeared into thin air?"

"Well, we've read enough mystery stories to know how to go about finding them. Let's try to figure out where they could be."

Diane's eyes sparkled as she turned and yanked open a desk drawer and pulled out a thick pad of yellow lined paper and a pencil.

"Sit down and help me reconstruct the scene. That's the first thing they do in books, you know." She drew a square box in the middle of the page and penciled in large letters Bedroom.

"Now, here's my mother's bed with the canopy over it, and here's the dresser. Over by the window is the big rocker." Diane sketched the furniture as she talked. "And over here by the window is the little blue vanity where my mother keeps her jewelry in the top drawer."

"But who would know expensive stuff was there?" Vickie objected. "I mean, if it was just a burglar, he would have searched everywhere and probably left things in a mess. He wouldn't just go right there to that drawer."

Diane sighed. "Vickie, *everybody* knows most women keep their jewelry in a dresser or vanity. I bet your mother does. And Francine."

"Well—yeah. My mother keeps hers in a locked jewelry

box in a drawer. And Francine doesn't wear very much jewelry. She has a couple of pieces that Pete gave her, but they're just costume jewelry, not very expensive. The only valuable things she has are a pearl ring and an old-fashioned watch on a thick, heavy gold chain that belonged to my great-grandmother. But even those she just keeps in a cut glass dish on top of her dresser. The dish is old too. It belonged to the same great—"

"But see? That proves my point," Diane interrupted. "Anybody who was going to steal jewelry would naturally look in those places first."

"Even so, that still doesn't give a clue as to who did it," Vickie objected. "Except—" She stopped. She wondered again if Mrs. Stewart had purposely lost them in order to get insurance money. But she could not say that to Diane. Then, answering Diane's questioning look, she went on slowly. "Except a person who would be able to go in and out of the bedroom and no one would pay any attention—"

Her voice trailed off as Diane sat up straight, her eyes flashing sparks. "If you think my mother is pretending about losing her bracelets!"

"No, not your mother," Vickie answered, feeling guilty for denying what she had wondered.

"Who then? Me?"

"Diane, don't be silly! Of course I don't mean you."

"Well, who then?"

"Well, I hate to say it, but doesn't that only leave Anna?"

"It—was—not—Anna!" Diane spaced the words emphatically.

Vickie turned on her in defense. "I know it's awful to think it, and I don't want to. But I can't be as positive as you are."

"The reason I am is because I was with her practically

85

every minute when she was here last week. I've been reading books to her, a couple of chapters each time she comes. That is, after I get my jobs done. You know how she always gives you jobs to do. She does me anyway. She always says, 'To know to clean good is to be good.'"

Diane imitated Anna's voice and accent so perfectly that Vickie had to laugh. But she sobered quickly and said, "The problem is convincing your mother that it was not Anna. Hey! Wait. What about one of the maintenance men? Did one of them come in to repair something?"

"Vickie! That's *awful* to accuse some poor innocent man of stealing."

Vickie stared back at Diane, hearing the fury in her voice. "I don't get it," she exclaimed. "I'm trying to figure out who could possibly have taken the bracelets, in order to get Anna off the hook, and you get mad at every suggestion I make."

"I suppose next you'll say the bracelets aren't really missing. I suppose you think we're just making up the whole thing. Well, I'll show you."

Diane stood up awkwardly. "Come on to my mother's room."

Vickie followed and watched Diane pull open a drawer in the little blue vanity and lift out a square green-velvet-covered jewel case. She turned around and held it for Vickie to see. "There. See? It's empty."

"How did you do that?" Vickie asked.

"What?"

"Open the case. You must have pressed something, since there isn't a key."

Diane looked back at her for a moment and then said irritably, "Honestly, Vickie, you should know that. *Anybody* knows that if there's no key for a jewelry box, then there has to be a secret spring of some kind. All you have to do is feel around for it."

She snapped the case shut. "Here, try it. Just run your finger carefully along the bottom edge, sort of at the back. What do you feel?"

Vickie took the case. "There's just a little—well, bump of some kind."

"OK. Press on it."

The top of the velvet-covered box opened as Vickie pushed gently on the tiny raised edge. She snapped it shut and then opened it again. Then, frowning down at the dainty box, she said, "But why wouldn't the thief just take the whole box? Wasn't there other stuff in it?"

Diane shook her head. "Not in this one. Just the bracelets were here. And he wouldn't take the box too because it would be too bulky in his pocket. You could wrap the bracelets in a handkerchief, and they wouldn't make your pocket stick out very much."

"Yeah, I guess," Vickie answered slowly, thinking without wanting to of the deep pockets in the apron Anna always wore.

She watched Diane put the jewelry case back into the drawer and followed her to her room. "Well, we aren't any closer to a solution now than when we started. And I'd better go home. Betty Lou will wonder where I am. Can you come over?"

Diane doodled circles across the bottom of the pad of paper, her face turned so that all Vickie could see was her mass of curls.

After a moment she asked, "Do you—really want me to come?"

Vickie stared at her. "What a crazy question! You know I do."

"But you and Betty Lou—"

"Diane! There's no law that says a person can have only one friend at a time."

"Yeah—but the two of you are always saying, 'Remember this' and 'Remember the time we did that,' things I don't know anything about. It makes me think you don't even know I'm there." Diane's voice sounded both angry and forlorn.

Knowing just how she felt, Vickie blurted an explanation. "That's only because I'm trying to keep her from missing her parents, especially her fath—"

She stopped abruptly and stared at Diane's fingers, motionless on the pencil she held, gripping tightly. How *dumb* to talk to Diane about missing her father. How could she forget the glimpse Diane had just given of how much her father's walking out had hurt her?

I've really blown it now, she told herself miserably. She watched Diane get up from the bed, her face turned away. She was sure Diane was hurt or angry or both as she stuck the pad of paper back in the desk drawer and slammed it shut.

But when she turned, her face was clear and her eyes crinkled in a smile. "OK, I'll come eat lunch with you guys."

Vickie let out her breath in a silent sigh of relief as she smiled back and pulled on her jacket. Diane scrawled a note for her mother.

"Naturally she'll know I'm with you, but I'd better leave a note anyhow."

Betty Lou was sitting on the floor watching TV when they got to the apartment. She looked up at them.

"Hi. I thought you two were doing something exciting, and I was missing out just because I was too lazy to get up."

"No. We were just sitting around trying to discover who

took my mother's bracelets," Diane answered. "We've decided it's an inside job."

"An inside job," Betty Lou repeated. "What's that?"

"That's police language for someone who thinks he won't be suspected of stealing, or whatever the crime is, because he is a trusted friend of the family."

Diane's voice was so superior sounding as she explained, that Betty Lou turned red. She looked quickly at Vickie and then away.

Remembering what Diane had said about Betty Lou's babyish name, Vickie thought impatiently, *She is awfully dumb about some things,* and then was angry at herself again for thinking that. Diane really did not have to sound so smart and so impatient when she talked to Betty Lou. She did not sound like that when she talked to anyone else.

"We didn't really decide that, Diane," she objected. "Neither one of us thinks it's Anna. You got mad when I wondered if it was a man come to fix something in your apartment and —"

"There are other people, you know, who could have done it."

"You mean, someone who lives on your floor?"

"Maybe." Diane stopped abruptly as though she had meant to say something else and looked away from the questioning frown on Vickie's face.

"Well, let's eat. I'm starved."

Vickie was hauling stuff out of the refrigerator when she heard the phone ring. Before she could grab the kitchen extension, her mother called from the den, "For you, Betty Lou. Long distance."

Betty Lou answered at the kitchen phone, and Vickie and Diane listened to her squeals as she talked, half laughing and half crying. When she hung up, she turned, bubbling. "The greatest news! My dad is lots better. He and Mom can fly back on Wednesday. That's day after tomorrow! And he has to stay home and can't travel for a couple of months. That means he'll be home every night instead of just on weekends the way he usually is."

Her voice ran on excitedly as they went back and forth taking food to the table at the sunny end of the dining room and then sat down to eat.

Suddenly Diane blurted, "Will you shut up? Just shut up!"

Vickie and Betty Lou stared at her and saw her face crumple and tears brim in her eyes. She jumped up from the table, dashed across the living room, through the hall to Vickie's room, and slammed the door. The lock clicked behind her.

"What's the matter with her?" Betty Lou demanded. "She sure is touchy. I can't say or do anything without her getting mad."

"Remember I told you her parents were divorced. It happened just around Christmas time. Usually she doesn't let on that it bothers her. But—"

Vickie stopped, hearing again the sound of Diane's voice, thick with years of held-back tears. She gestured helplessly. "But you see it does bother her very much." She stood up. "I'll go see if she'll come back."

"Tell her I'm awfully sorry," Betty Lou said contritely, following Vickie. "She doesn't like me anyhow, and this won't help any."

Vickie knocked hesitantly on the bedroom door. "Diane?"

"Go away!" Her voice came muffled, choked with tears.

"Diane, please let me in."

Mrs. Montgomery came from the den. "What's the matter?"

Vickie explained in a low voice, and Mrs. Montgomery

90

nodded understandingly. "Let me try." She knocked on the door. "Diane? May I come in, please?"

After a long moment of silence, Diane asked, "Can I wash my face first?"

"Of course. You'll find clean towels in the linen closet in the bathroom between Vickie's and Francine's rooms."

Mrs. Montgomery turned to Vickie and Betty Lou hovering anxiously behind her. "Girls, this is a very hard time for Diane just now with memories of her father's leaving. You go finish your lunch while I talk with her. It might help if you all were to get out of the apartment for the afternoon and do something active and interesting. What? Ski perhaps?"

"Great!" Betty Lou exclaimed.

But Vickie said quickly, "No, I'm sure Diane can't do that yet. The doctor won't let her do anything in gym even."

"What else would you suggest?"

"How about tobogganing? Can she do that?" Betty Lou asked.

"I don't know. Maybe."

"While I talk with Diane, you ask your father to see about renting toboggans for the afternoon if Diane can go." Mrs. Montgomery looked at them with a faint questioning smile. "You would not object to our going along?"

"How else would we get out to the slopes?" Vickie demanded and added, "Anyway, you guys are still fun to be with."

"Thanks!" Mrs. Montgomery retorted.

They waited anxiously outside the bedroom, listening to water running in the bathroom. Then they heard the tiny click as Diane unlocked the door. Mrs. Montgomery opened it and went in, closing the door firmly behind her.

When they came out a little later, Diane's eyes were red-rimmed and her face splotchy from tears. But she gave Betty Lou a faint, tired smile and mumbled, "Sorry I blew up. I'm really glad your dad is better."

Mr. Montgomery called from the den, "I've got us a couple of toboggans. Is it safe for you to go, Diane?"

"Yeah, I think so. If I don't get bumped around too much. You know, dumped out."

"We'll put you between us each time," he assured her.

"Invite your mother to go along," Mrs. Montgomery suggested.

Diane shook her head quickly. "She's not much for sports. Anyway, she just had her hair done—she won't want to get it all messed up."

The afternoon was fun. Vickie and Betty Lou saw a lot of people they knew from having been out to the slopes before, and Diane fit in with everyone. The cold, crisp air erased the anger that had flared in her. She seemed to have completely forgotten her blow-up at Betty Lou as she sledded down between her and Mr. Montgomery. When she trudged back up the hill with them, walking slowly and carefully, she talked animatedly with Betty Lou. Vickie watched them, glad that that problem was solved, even though the problem of the bracelets was not.

They stopped to eat on the way home. Mrs. Montgomery shook her head in pretended disgust that the girls preferred hamburgers and french fries to "all that leftover turkey in the refrigerator."

"Oh, well, Pete will help get rid of that," Vickie said.

"That's what we're afraid of," her father retorted. "We've got to get home and get our share."

When they got back to the apartment building, Vickie and Betty Lou pushed through the doors with Diane into her lobby and waited until she got on the elevator. The

Montgomerys waited in the courtyard near the fountain, looking up at the surrounding trees glittering with a blaze of colored lights. They were deep in conversation as Vickie and Betty Lou crossed toward them. Vickie saw the serious expression on her father's face that meant he was really worried about something. She saw him shake his head at something Mrs. Montgomery said. Then his voice came clearly in the still cold air.

"I've begun to suspect that too," he answered. "But how can we help her without hurting her more?"

Uneasiness gripped Vickie. They could only be talking about the missing jewelry. Since it was Anna who needed help, they must be talking about her. "I've begun to suspect that, too," her father had said. That must mean he had changed his mind and now thought Anna was guilty.

That meant she and Diane simply *had* to find those bracelets—and do it fast. Her mind turned the problem over and over as they rode up in the elevator and waited while Mr. Montgomery unlocked the apartment door.

"Hi, you all!"

Francine came from her room, toweling her hair dry. "Apparently I missed some fun." She looked at them in their warm clothes and boots, their cheeks still flushed from the cold, and shook her head. "That's what comes of being a working girl. *I* can't knock off work any time I want to the way *some* people I know do."

She smiled at her father who answered, "I'm a working person too, just remember. But fortunately, not many people are thinking about lawyers the day after Christmas."

Except Mrs. Stewart and Anna, Vickie said silently.

Francine turned back into her room, then stopped and called over her shoulder, "Mother? Did you borrow my watch? You know—your grandmother's?"

"No," Mrs. Montgomery called back from the hall. "Why?"

"Pete is taking me to meet his parents when they fly in tomorrow and have dinner with them in the hotel where they are staying. I decided to wear that watch with my ruffled blouse. I want to impress his mother that I'm both old-fashioned and modern. Think that will do it?"

"Be sure to tell her that you know how to bake bread," Mrs. Montgomery retorted, smiling back at her affectionately. "Are you bringing them here after dinner so we can meet them?"

"Yes, if they're still interested in meeting the family after they meet me."

"If Pete isn't worried about their liking you, you needn't be," her mother assured her and then added, "Now, what is this about your watch?"

"Well, since we're going to dinner right after work tomorrow, I wanted to get everything laid out tonight and be ready. But my watch isn't in the usual place. I thought maybe you had borrowed it."

Mrs. Montgomery shook her head. "Not I."

"Vickie?" Francine's voice was questioning, though she added quickly, "I know you don't usually take things without permission—except for makeup, of course," she added with a smile.

Vickie made a face back at her, remembering how she had looked that day last summer when she had slathered on Francine's makeup, trying to disguise herself.

"I wouldn't borrow anything as valuable as your watch. I'd be afraid I'd lose it."

Vickie turned suddenly and saw the strange look on her mother's face as she stood in the doorway of Francine's room. Her voice was slow as though she were forcing out the words. "When did you last wear the watch?"

Francine shrugged her shoulders. "Oh—I don't remember. I don't usually wear it just for everyday, you know. And I guess when I don't wear it I don't think about it. It's just always been right here in this lovely old dish that belonged to your grandmother. That's why I keep it there, I guess—just for sentimental reasons. The pearl ring is there and a few other pieces that I seldom wear, but not the watch."

She stopped, frowning in thought. "Why would the watch be missing and nothing else? I'm sure I would have put it back there whenever I last wore it."

She stopped abruptly, looking across the room at Mrs. Montgomery. "You don't suppose—"

Vickie looked from her mother to Francine and then back again, sure she could read the thought that neither had yet put into words. She felt sick. Anna again.

Then Francine shook her head. "I'm not going to believe it. There has to be some other explanation. Maybe I did put it somewhere else. Or maybe I even lost it. I'm going to believe that first before I will believe that Anna took it."

Vickie heard her mother saying something in return. But she stood motionless as an even worse thought pushed its way into her mind. She had just been talking to Diane about the watch, and now it was gone. And Diane had been locked in her bedroom earlier today, right next to Francine's room.

Then she shook her head. No, the thought was impossible. Diane would not steal. And she certainly would not steal her own mother's jewelry. And if she had, she would have put it back when she found out her mother was blaming Anna.

Besides, Diane was not the only one who had been

alone in the bedroom today. Betty Lou had been there by herself all morning.

Then, out of the mist of questions and doubts swirling around her, one scene came clearly. She saw again Betty Lou in the store, the yarn pulled from the bag she carried, and the store detective's stern, accusing eyes.

And, as Vickie half listened to her parents and Francine, not meeting Betty Lou's eyes, another memory came. This memory was from last year, from sixth grade gym class. Miss Becker had missed money from her desk one day after Betty Lou had used the telephone. But nothing had been done because everyone knew Betty Lou had no reason to steal.

Now the question was inescapable—was Betty Lou a thief?

9

Anger surged in Vickie then and disgust at herself for her disloyalty. How could she suspect her two best friends? She stood without moving, caught in conflicting emotions.

This whole thing was like a giant puzzle. Odd-shaped pieces lay in a clutter—pieces that ought to fit and yet did not. She frowned in concentration. If only she had time to sort through them all, perhaps she could find one central unifying piece, and then all the others would fall into place around it. But was there such a piece? What if they never did find the right answer and Anna was forever branded a thief?

Her parents and Francine had gone on talking. She brought her attention back to them.

"Well, at least Anna can't be blamed for this," Francine said. "She didn't clean here today."

Her father answered quietly, "Remember, Francine, you don't really know when your watch was taken. You said you don't remember when you last wore it."

"But—but I would have noticed before now that it was missing. I distinctly remember wearing it last Sunday— that is, a week ago Sunday, when Pete took me to the concert."

"And Anna came to clean last Tuesday morning."

Mrs. Montgomery's words dropped into a pool of silence, and they all stared at one another.

Then Vickie said absently, "Afternoon."

When they turned to look at her, she repeated, "Afternoon. Anna always cleans for Mrs. Stewart Tuesday mornings."

Mrs. Montgomery shook her head. "Usually, yes. But last week she was here in the morning. Don't you remember my telling you that?" She looked at Vickie as she asked the question. "You asked about her when you came home from school Tuesday afternoon while I was baking the last batch of cookies—"

She broke off, frowned a moment in thought, and then went on. "Oh, you didn't know about the change in plans. I started to tell you, and then I was afraid the cookies were getting too brown, and I hurried to take the pan out of the oven and didn't finish my explanation. Anna had asked if she could clean for me in the morning that day." She hesitated for a moment before saying, "Mrs. Stewart did not go to work that day because she was taking Diane to the doctor in the afternoon. Anna preferred not to work there while Mrs. Stewart was home."

Vickie stared back at her mother and felt her mind scrambling like a squirrel in a trap. Part of the evidence Diane was going to use to prove that Anna was not guilty was that she had been with Anna every minute that day when she had cleaned. She was going to say that she had followed Anna around, reading a book to her. But she had not. She had not been there. She had been at the doctor's office all afternoon.

I've got to get to her right away and remind her of that, she told herself frantically. *It will only make it harder for Anna if Diane makes up evidence, and then everyone finds out it isn't true.*

Then the thought that the only solid clue they had to Anna's innocence was gone made her blurt out, "It wasn't

Anna! It wasn't! You know she wouldn't steal."

She had said those words so many times that even to her ears they now sounded hollow.

Without paying any attention to her outburst, Mrs. Montgomery asked again, "Francine, could you have lost the watch and not noticed it? Could the chain have broken?"

Francine shook her head. "No. Of course, I don't actually remember taking it off and putting it away, because that's the kind of thing a person does automatically."

She stopped and half smiled. "Anyway, that Sunday I was too busy thinking about Pete and what a good time we had had." She sobered and went on. "But you know what a heavy chain it is. And since it doesn't have a clasp, but just slips over my head, it couldn't have fallen off accidentally."

"You have looked carefully in your room?" her father asked again. "Are you absolutely sure you did not just put it in a drawer that evening—while you were thinking about Pete—instead of back in its usual place?" He made his voice sound like a lawyer questioning a witness, though a faint smile accompanied his legal tone.

"No, sir," she answered him back seriously like a witness in court. "Unless I hid it for some reason I can't remember and then blanked out, it is not anywhere in my room."

Vickie saw the troubled look on her mother's face and watched her reach with both hands to rub her forehead. "Francine, it simply *must* be here. I will help you look tomorrow. But right now, every bone and muscle in me is crying out for a hot bath and a soft bed."

Mr. Montgomery glanced at his watch and nodded agreement. "I am going to turn in also. I have a rough day ahead of me tomorrow. I promised Anna I would come home early enough so that she could talk to me here rather than having her come down to the office."

He stopped and looked questioningly at his wife. "Will she be here in the afternoon as usual?"

She nodded. "Yes, it was only for last week that she asked for the change."

Vickie expected to be so tired from walking up the toboggan slopes that she would go right to sleep. Instead, she found herself edgy, unable to get into a comfortable position. She turned her pillow repeatedly, thumping it into a bunched heap under her head and then tugging it out straight. She envied Betty Lou's ability to go to sleep almost as soon as she crawled into bed. But of course Betty Lou's mind was not churning over the bracelets— and now the watch—because she was not involved. Naturally, not knowing Anna, Betty Lou did not understand how serious this was. Anna was so honest and so proud that even when they proved she was not guilty, she would still be terribly hurt just to have been suspected. And now Anna was coming tomorrow. What could she say to make Anna feel better and take away this terrible hurt? And how could they even prove she was innocent unless they found the bracelets?

The sleepless night made her tense the next morning when she woke to the sound of the phone ringing.

"Honestly, that phone!" she muttered crossly, as she shoved off the blanket and groped for her slippers. "Every morning it rings. Great vacation this is," she fumed as she peered at the clock.

So what if it was ten o'clock and past time to be up? It still was annoying to have the phone wake you practically every morning of vacation.

She closed the bedroom door, hurried out to the

kitchen, and reached for the note propped against the toaster, the writing done in her mother's familiar straight up-and-down script.

"Back this afternoon with Dad," was all it said. No word about where she was. Vickie grabbed the phone before it could ring again and heard Diane say, "Vickie? I've had a sign in the window for a couple of hours. Whatcha been doing?"

Vickie yawned. Nothing seemed terribly urgent this morning when she was half dead for sleep. "I just woke up," she answered. "I hardly have my eyes open yet," she said as she stretched on tiptoe in the kitchen doorway to get a glimpse of Diane's window.

Then last night's events rushed back and she snapped alive. "Hey, Diane, I've got to talk to you. We have a complication in our evidence about Anna. Can you come over?"

"Yeah, but tell me now."

"I don't want to tell you on the phone. Come on over and we can talk before Betty Lou gets up. My mother's gone, but she's coming back before Anna gets through working. And this is about her. Anna, I mean."

Diane's voice came back, thin and strained. "Anna isn't coming to clean for us this morning. If she's going to be at your place, maybe I shouldn't be there. She probably won't want to see me."

"Well, can't you just tell her that you don't agree with your mother? You haven't changed your mind, have you?"

"No!"

She almost yelled the word, and made Vickie pull the receiver away from her ear. With Diane that positive, it was too bad she could not convince her mother. The trouble was that the most important part of her evidence was not true. And now, added to the puzzle of the bracelets, was Francine's missing watch.

She thought about the whole mess as she dressed quickly in the bathroom without disturbing Betty Lou. The trouble was that there just was not a long enough list of suspects. She still felt ashamed of her quick suspicion about Diane and Betty Lou. But unless someone was roaming around the apartment building with keys to individual apartments, Anna was the only one to suspect. How could their trust in Anna be right when all the facts seemed to show that they were wrong?

She was fixing cereal and hot chocolate when Diane knocked her usual broken-rhythm signal on the door. Vickie opened it and Diane limped in slowly, wincing as she eased herself down onto a dining room chair.

"I guess I sort of twisted something yesterday," she answered Vickie's questioning look. "But I'm glad I went. It was fun."

"Listen, I've got to tell you something while we eat. And quick, before Betty Lou comes out or Anna comes."

"Well, what?"

Vickie thought quickly. Which should she tell first? Probably reminding Diane of the change in the cleaning plans was more important than telling about Francine's missing watch. So she blurted, "Diane, Anna didn't clean at your place last Tuesday morning."

"What do you mean? She always cleans for us Tuesday morning and for you in the afternoon." Diane reached for a piece of toast as she answered, not looking at Vickie.

"But she didn't last week," Vickie insisted. "For some reason, she asked my mother if she could switch. It wouldn't make any difference except that if you said you were with her all the time she was there, it wouldn't be true. You were at the doctor all afternoon."

Vickie watched Diane's face go white and a hunted look creep into her eyes. She added quickly, "I wanted to remind you before you told anyone else you were home with Anna. Now we've got to find some other way of proving that Anna is innocent."

After a moment, Diane nodded and lifted her shoulders in a helpless gesture. "Yeah, you're right. I wasn't there. But I didn't think anyone else would know or remember about her switching times. I suppose your mother remembered?"

Vickie nodded.

"I wouldn't have—have lied about it, if it hadn't been so important to help Anna. I mean, since she didn't take the bracelets, the lie was for a good reason."

Vickie listened, knowing her father would say there was never any good reason to lie, but decided not to argue with Diane.

"Something else has happened," she began, but stopped at the sound of a key turning in the front door lock, and Anna's voice calling, "Yoo-hoo. I am here."

Diane looked across at Vickie and bit her lip. "I wish I hadn't come. I know she'll hate me."

"She won't either," Vickie snapped back and jumped up to answer Anna. She bumped into Betty Lou coming from the bedroom, rubbing her eyes and yawning.

"I've saved you breakfast, and Diane and I are still eating."

Vickie tossed the words in Betty Lou's direction and went past her into the wide front hall. "Hi, Anna. You've got three of us to help you clean today." She could hear the rushed, nervous, overly friendly sound of her voice.

"So. You have friends who come to visit."

Anna took off her heavy coat and hung it away in the closet. Then she leaned to pull the big apron from the shopping bag she had set on the floor by the door. The apron completely covered her clothes and tied on each side of her wide waist. It had deep pockets all around in which she put dustcloths and other cleaning equipment. In spite of this, the apron stuck out all around her, so starched stiff that Vickie and Diane laughed about how dirt would slide right off it.

"You're our creature from outer space," Diane said once affectionately.

"Yah. It is enough to be in this space," Anna had retorted.

Vickie watched Anna tie the apron and then said, "Diane is here and another friend I've known all my life."

She led the way through the hall and kitchen to the dining room and introduced Betty Lou. Anna nodded her head at her and then gave Diane a faint smile. She looked at Vickie. "I was not still here when you get home last week. I not hear how you like your mama's tree."

They trailed her back to the den where Anna stood in the middle of the room, hands on her hips as she looked at the tree. "It is beautiful, no?"

"It's lots nicer than ours."

Vickie heard the high, nervous sound of Diane's voice as she stood poised in the doorway.

Anna did not look around. "Yours, it is nice too. But Vickie's mama she is an artist. For her, all must be perfect. And yet—"

She stopped, lips pursed, her head to one side as she studied the tree. "And yet it is not like a picture in a magazine only. It is part of herself she puts into it. Part of her heart."

In the silence she turned briskly. "I start now." She looked sharply at them as they stood facing her, clustered in the doorway. "So you want to help. I must see how you do jobs."

"Anna."

Vickie looked quickly at Diane, caught by the urgency of her voice. She had moved away from the doorway and stood leaning against the soft brown leather of the big desk chair. Her thin face was pale under her curls, although her cheeks were flushed as though she had a fever. From where she stood, Vickie could see that Diane's hands were clenched behind her, her finger nails digging into the palms of her hands.

Diane swallowed before she spoke again, still in a high, nervous voice so unlike her usual lilt. "Anna. I'm sorry about—about what is happening. I didn't know my mother would blame you. I told her it wasn't you, but she wouldn't listen."

Anna, standing solid in the middle of the room, looked back at her. "Yah. For thirty years I have cleaned for ladies. Not one time has someone said to me, 'Anna, you are a thief.' When I see so much as a penny on the floor, I pick it up and put it *so*."

She stooped over for an imaginery piece of money, straightened, and slapped her hand down on the desk.

"You could not pay me enough money so that I should steal. Better I should starve first."

Diane flew across the room and threw her arms around Anna's wide waist. Tears streamed down her face. "I told my mother it wasn't you. I told her," she repeated.

"There, there." Anna put one arm around Diane. Her voice was gentle as she answered, "You are not to worry. Vickie's papa will see to it. He makes bad things come straight."

Vickie heard the words, but was not reassured. She could not help asking herself, *What if Dad can't help her?*

What will we do if the bracelets are never found? What will happen to Anna then?

But Anna was moving briskly again, her voice full of its usual scolding affection. "Now we work." She kept one work-roughened hand on Diane, gently rubbing her shoulders as she gave directions.

"Vickie, you will again see to the polishing of silver. Your Mama had out the fancy forks and spoons for the big party. She will want them soon again."

She nodded at Betty Lou. "You, I do not know how you work. Is it good or bad?"

"Not too good," Betty Lou replied, caught up in the honesty of the moment.

"Then you polish tables. When we see faces, we know you do good."

She handed them cleaning and polishing cloths before turning to look at Diane. Her voice was gentle as she asked, "So, you must still wear your back holder? It does not yet come off?"

Diane moved back and looked up into Anna's face. "No, the doctor said I have to wear it a couple more months."

"He promised then you will stand straight with no hurt?"

Vickie stood motionless, caught by the tenderness in Anna's voice, the loving concern that looked from her eyes. Diane had been afraid Anna would turn from her. She had not. Instead, Anna acted as though Diane were a bird with a broken wing who needed special care.

Anna handed Diane a bottle of cleaning solution and a roll of soft paper. "For you today, clean mirrors. For that you must stretch but not too much. It is just right exercise for you."

She looked from one to the other like a general marshaling his troops and said, "Now we work."

Anna led the way with her usual vigorous cleaning of carpets and draperies and furniture. But on the way in and out of rooms, she stopped with words of caution to Betty Lou. "You must rub so to see your face in the shine." And to Vickie, "Do not be stingy with the soap and water or your papa will eat polish with his potatoes."

"There. I'm finished," Diane said. "What shall I do next?"

"First I inspect," Anna replied.

After Diane had repolished two mirrors in the bathroom, Anna said, "Now to help me with the clean sheets will be good. We start here in Mama's and Papa's room."

"Are you going to flip the mattresses today too?"

"For sure," Vickie heard Anna answer firmly.

Diane called, "Vickie, you and Betty Lou better come help Anna with this mattress. It's too big and heavy for her to do alone."

Vickie smiled to herself. It had not taken Diane long to bounce back to her usual self, taking charge of everybody and everything. But you could never get mad about it because she always did it to help, not just to be bossy.

They finally managed to heave over the king-sized mattress, with Anna cautioning Diane not to lift.

"OK," she agreed. "But maybe I can help on Vickie's twin beds since they're lighter."

Anna shook her head. "The two girls lift there. Diane— only watch."

They trooped into Vickie's room and Diane said, "Okay, since I can't do this fun part of flipping the mattress over, I'll yank off the sheets, and you two can do the turning. Here, do yours first, Vickie."

Vickie and Betty Lou pulled and lifted and shoved until they finally flipped it over. Anna came then and deftly stripped the sheets from the other bed. "Better I should help or I not be finished when your mama comes."

She took hold of one side of the mattress in her strong hands and lifted it as they all moved over to help.

But as Anna raised the mattress, she stopped. They all stood motionless beside her, staring down at the pile of gold that lay in the middle of the bed under the mattress. Vickie caught her breath as she saw the two gold bracelets and the gold watch in the middle of the crumpled golden pile of heavy chain.

"It's your mother's bracelets! And Francine's watch!"

"But how did they get there?" Betty Lou cried. "That's the bed I've been sleeping in!"

Betty Lou looked around at them, her face repeating the question her voice had asked. Then she stared at Diane.

Vickie, looking around at Betty Lou, saw the expression on her face change from surprise to fear as she looked at Diane.

Diane exclaimed triumphantly, "I told you Anna didn't do it. Anna, I told everyone that I knew you hadn't taken those things. I knew all along it was someone else!"

10

In the silence that followed Diane's triumphant cry, came the sound of the front door's opening. "Girls, we're home," Mrs. Montgomery called.

The thoughts, doubts, and anxieties tumbling in Vickie's mind kept her from answering. She stood still, staring down at the incriminating pile of jewelry. Had it lain hidden under the mattress all this time while they looked for it and talked about it? Here under the mattress of the bed where Betty Lou had been sleeping all week? Even though she tried to push away the memory of the ugly scene in the store, it came again, crowding into her mind, coloring her feelings about Betty Lou.

Betty Lou had been in tears when the store detective accused her of stealing. She had been convincing as she protested her innocence.

And I believed her because I thought I knew her. But now—here was proof that could not be talked away. And yet—how could she turn on Betty Lou when they had been friends so long?

"What are you all doing?" Mrs. Montgomery asked from the bedroom doorway.

Vickie faced her parents as they came into the room and motioned with her hand, not answering.

"You all look like statues standing here—" Mrs. Montgomery broke off her laughing comment as she too stared down at the pile of gold pieces.

Then Diane bent swiftly and picked up the bracelets. "You see? These are my mother's. I knew Anna hadn't taken them. I just knew it. We know she didn't because we were right here with her when she lifted the mattress and found them. The stuff was already here and she was just as surprised as we were." She looked around at them and then leaned to pick up the watch. "I knew she hadn't taken Francine's watch either."

Vickie stood silent, listening to Diane's insistence on Anna's innocence. She was glad for the proof that would clear Anna. But a terrible, miserable feeling began to grow inside her. The facts were beginning to shape into a pattern that she did not want to admit even to herself. That one big clue to the puzzle stared at her and she fought against admitting it, hating to have to spell it out for everyone to know.

Betty Lou protested again, her voice shaky and clouded with tears. "I don't know how all this got under my mattress. *I* didn't put any of it there."

She stared around at the circle of them looking at her and repeated, "I didn't!"

Diane spoke slowly, her voice showing her regret. "I didn't think you really had taken that yarn in the store either. But now—" she left the sentence unfinished.

"I didn't do that either!" Betty Lou's voice shook now with anger. "Vickie, you know I wouldn't steal anything. Why should I? My folks give me everything I want."

Mr. Montgomery's quiet voice interrupted. "I suggest that we let Anna get on with her work so that she will not be delayed in leaving."

He turned to her. "I do not believe you will require my services now. Mrs. Stewart will say no more to you about this."

Anna nodded. "I am glad. To be called a thief, it is not good."

Mr. Montgomery went on, his voice still quiet. "My wife and I want you to know that we never once believed you were involved in this. We do not have all the answers yet, but at least your mind can be at rest. We will handle this with Mrs. Stewart so that you do not need to speak to her about it. Whether or not you go back there to clean—"

"That I will not," Anna broke in. "I would not be easy in my mind even one day." She looked past him to the girls lined motionless along the bed.

Then Vickie saw Anna and her parents exchange a silent message, and there was troubled concern on Anna's face as she said, "For the little one who has the trouble, you will help?"

"She will need a great deal of help from everyone who loves her, Anna, including you," Mrs. Montgomery answered.

Anna nodded, seeming to understand the message that lay behind the spoken words, and turned to finish making the bed.

Diane begged, "Oh, please, Anna! Please don't quit coming to clean for us. I know my mother will be sorry she blamed you."

Anna reached to pat her shoulder. "Wait to see," she answered gently.

Mr. Montgomery turned to the girls. "Perhaps we should go back to the den and talk this through."

"Well, it doesn't really matter who did it or how the stuff got here under the mattress now that we know Anna didn't do it," Diane said, slipping the bracelets on one slender arm. "That was all we had to prove. My mother won't care who took the bracelets as long as she gets them back."

Vickie looked at Diane, puzzling over the difference in

the sound of her voice. A few minutes ago when she had pounced on the discovered jewelry, her voice had been happy. No, more than that—she had sounded triumphant, as though she had been proved right about something she had been sure of all the time. But now she did not seem at all interested in the solution to the mystery. She acted as though it were not important anymore. Maybe it was because she did not want to make things worse for Betty Lou.

Vickie knew her father had sensed the difference in Diane's attitude too, because he asked, "Don't you think we *should* care? True, Anna did not take the bracelets, but someone did. That someone should be discovered—and helped. Let's sit down for a few minutes and talk about it."

Mr. Montgomery led the way into the den and sat down at his desk, while they dropped onto the edge of chairs, facing him. He looked at each of them in turn, his eyes serious, his hands clasped loosely in front of him on the clear glass top of the big desk.

Vickie watched him, wondering how he knew what to do to unravel this mystery. Maybe he did not know, but was only hoping he could ask the right questions and stumble onto the right answers. Then she mentally shook her head at that idea. He had not become a famous lawyer by accidentally solving cases. But she wondered, did he suspect the one fact about this case that she knew, the fact she would not tell unless she was forced to? She darted a quick look at Betty Lou, who sat staring at the floor, and then at Diane sitting relaxed, twirling the glittering bracelets on her arm.

Mr. Montgomery cleared his throat and said, "Perhaps working together we can line up all the facts that we have. First of all, we can be glad that a person's innocence has been proved. That does not always happen even though

112

our legal system tries to be just. Sometimes an innocent person is trapped by evidence that is only circumstantial but seems impossible to disprove."

"Oh, but that wouldn't have happened this time," Diane burst out impulsively. "We *knew* Anna hadn't done it."

Mr. Montgomery looked at her in silence for a moment. Then he said gently, "Not all of us knew that as a fact, Diane. We all *believed* it, of course, but there is a difference in knowing someone is not guilty and in believing he is not. At least that is true in this case." He stopped and then asked, "Isn't that so, Diane?"

His voice was still quiet and gentle, but now it was probing also. Vickie listened, staring down at her hands tightly gripped in her lap, not wanting to look at either Betty Lou or Diane.

Diane looked back at him without answering. A puzzled frown creased her forehead as she tried to follow his meaning.

Mr. Montgomery went on. "The facts seem to be that you, Vickie, and you, Betty Lou, were at Diane's the evening the jewelry was later discovered to be missing. Were all three of you together every minute of that time?"

"You're thinking about an alibi, aren't you?" Diane's eyes were sparkling as she asked. Then she answered his question quickly. "Most of the time we were together playing games in the bedroom. Except I went out to the kitchen to get us something to eat. I think though—" She stopped, frowning at the memory, and then went on. "Yes, I'm sure Vickie came out to the kitchen to help me carry stuff."

Yes. Diane had insisted on her help. Vickie remembered that.

Her father asked, "Leaving Betty Lou alone? By your mother's open bedroom door?"

"Well—y-yes," Diane admitted slowly, her voice shaded with regret as she slanted a quick glance at Betty Lou. "She did say something when we came back about how pretty. my mother's room was—"

"I just looked in the door! I didn't go in! Mr. Montgomery, I didn't—"

He stopped Betty Lou's tearful protest with a movement of his hand. Then he looked at Vickie. "Were you with one of the others all evening, every minute?"

"Well, I—I went into the bathroom once."

His gaze went back to Diane. "Your apartment is like ours, is it not? The bathroom is between the two bedrooms with a door opening into each room from it? You and your mother share the bath the way Vickie and Francine do?"

"Yes, but—"

Without paying any attention to Diane's answer, he went on, "So that Vickie was alone for several minutes also, near the room where the jewelry was. It would have taken her only a minute or two, with the bathroom door locked, to slip into your mother's room—"

"Dad!"

"You can't think Vickie would steal!" Diane protested.

"Why not?" he asked. "How can you be sure she wouldn't?"

"Well, because Vickie is Vickie. And besides, we know Betty Lou had already tried to take something in the store."

"I did not!"

Mr. Montgomery did not even look at Betty Lou as the loud, angry words burst out. His eyes studied Diane for a moment before he said, "I believe it was you who suggested at the time that the yarn had simply fallen into the shopping bag Betty Lou was carrying."

A slight note of desperation crept into Diane's voice as

she answered him. "Well, I-I thought that must have been what happened. I mean—I didn't think any friend of Vickie's would steal. So that's why I said that. But then—then my mother's jewelry disappeared after she had been over with Vickie. So—" She stopped, her thin fingers restlessly turning the bracelets on her wrist.

"So that is the reason you were so sure Anna had not taken the bracelets?" he asked, his eyes steady on her face. "You believed Betty Lou had?"

"Well—y-yes."

It was like a duel between them, Vickie thought. Hearing her father's quiet but relentless voice, she could understand why he was so respected—and so feared by the guilty —because of his step-by-step, careful development of evidence.

"And then, when I heard Francine's watch was missing and—and it happened while Betty Lou was visiting, well—" Diane threw her hands out in a regretful gesture.

"Yes," Mr. Montgomery nodded. "We come to Francine's watch."

Vickie stared down at the floor, knowing he was going to ask the question she had been dreading the last few minutes, the question she would have to answer.

"Vickie. When did you tell Diane that Francine's watch was missing?"

This was the clue that would unravel the puzzle for them, but it was the fact that would hurt Diane. She shook her head as they all turned to look at her. Her voice was a whisper in the quiet room. "I didn't tell her."

Diane turned, her face white, her voice sharp. "You did too! You told me all about it. I remember exactly what you said. You said it was a watch that belonged to your great-grandmother. You even told me where she kept—it." Her voice trailed off as she finished the sentence, and she slumped back against the chair.

Still carefully avoiding looking at Diane, Vickie said, her voice low, almost pleading, "I told you about Francine having the watch when I was at your house yesterday morning. I told you where she kept it. But I didn't tell you the watch was missing. We didn't know it was gone until last night when we got back from tobogganing." Her voice trembled into silence.

Mrs. Montgomery spoke then and her voice, like her husband's, was quiet and gentle and very sad.

"Diane, dear. When you were here yesterday, locked in Vickie's room in tears, you had ample time to go into Francine's room and take the watch from its place on her dresser. Did you put it under Betty Lou's mattress then in order to make her look guilty? And is that where your mother's bracelets have been all this time?"

Vickie's throat ached from the tears she tried to hold back. She looked across the quiet room at Diane, her friend. Diane's thin face was defiant under the questioning look on Mrs. Montgomery's face. Her lips twisted as she tried to form words in answer. Then she put up both hands to cover her face, and Vickie saw tears seep through her fingers.

In the awkward silence, Betty Lou stood up. "I'd better start packing. It will take me a while to get all my stuff together." She passed Diane and lightly touched her shoulder on the way out the door.

The touch made Diane cry harder, and they could barely understand her words.

"I'm s-sorry. I g-guess I was j-jealous of B-Betty Lou. She and V-Vickie k-kept t-talking—about things I d-didn't know anything about. They had so m-many years of f-fun things to remember. And—and—I—I f-felt so left out!"

116

I know what that feeling is like, Vickie thought. *And it's awful.*

Diane fought for control, groping for the handkerchief Mrs. Montgomery put in her lap. She finally went on talking in a quieter voice. "I really didn't have anything against Betty Lou. And I really didn't mean to hurt her." She lifted her eyes for a moment, begging for their understanding.

"I guess I didn't stop to think what a terrible thing I was doing to her. But I was jealous because I didn't want Vickie to like her better than m-me. I've never had a friend like V-Vickie—someone who was always the same, someone I could count on no matter what. I knew lots of kids in grade school, but none of them were friends the way Vickie is."

She stopped, gulping back the tears that trembled her voice again. "But sometimes I couldn't stand to come over here. You—you're all so *nice* to each other. You never fight—never yell—"

Vickie's throat ached with pity as she glimpsed the hurt in Diane. So that was why Diane always said, "You come over to my house," when they planned to do things together. How could she have been with Diane constantly for the last six months and not seen the pain and loneliness that lay behind the smile she always wore?

Bits of remembered conversations flooded her mind, and she thought, *Anna saw it.* Her mother had said, way back the day Christmas vacation began, before all this happened, that Anna thought Diane's spirit hurt more than her body did. This was what she had meant.

Vickie forced her attention back to Diane, her voice small and ashamed as she went on with her explanation.

"That day in the store I really dropped the yarn in the bag as a joke. I meant to tease Betty Lou about taking it, but then the store detective saw it and was so awful to Betty Lou.

I didn't stop to think that anybody would think it was shoplifting." She looked quickly at Vickie and then away.

"Then, later on, when—when I saw—" She stopped and started again. "I didn't plan to do anything bad to Betty Lou, cause trouble for her. I just—just wanted Vickie to see that she wasn't so great after all. When I saw how easy it was to—to blame someone for something, that's when I decided to take the bracelets and put them where it would look like she had taken them." Her voice pleaded for understanding.

"When did you put them under the mattress?" Mr. Montgomery asked.

"Last Friday. I had them in my jacket pocket in a handkerchief the day I brought Vickie's present over."

The scene came back to Vickie. Diane fumbling in her jacket pocket for a Kleenex for her nose, herself trying to grab the jacket, and Diane fending her off. She had been in the bedroom alone after she had made fun of the manger scene. Then later, when she and Diane had talked, Diane had explained how a smart burglar would take the bracelets out of the case and wrap them in a handkerchief to keep his pocket from bulging. She had thought how clever Diane was to think of that. But she had thought of it because she had already done it.

Diane was talking again, haltingly. "After I took the bracelets, I knew I shouldn't have done it, that it was wrong to hurt Betty Lou like that. So I decided to come get them and put them someplace where my mother would sort of accidentally find them. Sometimes she does mislay things when she's been—"

Diane broke off the sentence abruptly, but the word she had intended to say hung unspoken in the room. It brought back to Vickie the image of Mrs. Stewart stumbling and slurring her speech.

"I was going to get them when we came to your open

house on the way to the airport. My mother was wearing her mink coat and it has an extra deep pocket on one side. I thought I could drop the bracelets in it, and she'd find them and think she had left them there. But I didn't have a chance to get them. Betty Lou was in the bedroom the whole time with Susie and the kitten. There was no way I could slide my hand under the mattress and yank them out. So I thought maybe I could get them Monday. And then I heard my mother blaming Anna. I didn't think she would do that. I tried and tried to make her see that Anna wouldn't steal, but she wouldn't listen to me."

"And you could not bring yourself to tell her the truth." Mr. Montgomery's voice was stern.

Diane looked at him across the room and said simply, "No, sir. I wasn't brave enough."

I wouldn't be brave enough to confess something to Mrs. Stewart either, Vickie thought. Looking at her father, she was sure he understood.

But all he said was, "Go on."

"So I had to figure out some way to prove that Anna didn't take the bracelets, and I had to do it quick before my mother talked to the police. But I couldn't think of anything until Vickie told me about Francine's watch."

Diane darted a quick glance at Mrs. Montgomery. "Yes, you're right. I stuck it under Betty Lou's mattress yesterday when I was in Vickie's room. I knew Anna would clean today, and I thought if we were all there when she turned over the mattress, well, it would show she hadn't taken the things. I mean, they would already be there."

"What would you have done if she hadn't turned the mattresses?"

"I just thought she would. She always does at our house."

Vickie listened, understanding why Diane had been so insistent about all of them helping Anna with a job she usually did by herself with no trouble. It was funny how you did not notice little things like that at the time. But it was the almost overlooked little clues that were so important in solving mysteries.

Diane was talking, her voice low and broken again. "I've felt so awful all week. I've never done anything sneaky like this before. I don't know why I did it now. But ever since I've had this thing with my back, I get so—so jittery and uptight over things. And I get mad so quick over nothing. I never used to. I don't know what's wrong with me."

Diane fumbled in her jeans pocket for another handkerchief as Mrs. Montgomery moved swiftly to sit down beside her on the arm of the chair and give her a comforting hug.

Diane's voice was rough with tears again as she went on compulsively explaining. "I'm really sorry for what I've done to Betty Lou. I knew it wasn't her fault that I was jealous, but I couldn't stop how I felt. I wanted Vickie to like me better than anyone else. Then once I started this, it just got bigger, even when I tried to fix it. I had to choose between hurting Betty Lou and hurting Anna. I couldn't let anything happen to Anna. When she's at our house, we talk. She listens—and she understands things."

"But you see, you only succeeded in getting yourself in deeper. And you have hurt Anna whether you intended to or not. And, of course, this was a terrible hurt to Betty Lou." Mr. Montgomery was still stern.

Diane nodded. Her thin hands came up again, covering her face.

Mr. Montgomery looked around at them, and now when he spoke, his voice was tired, heavy sounding.

"I think perhaps we have all learned a lesson from this. Not one of us is immune from the temptation to do something that he knows is wrong. One lie almost always demands another to cover the first one, and then another. I hope you girls will learn that now while you are young."

Diane's voice quavered as she said, "My mother says I have been terrible to live with ever since this scoliosis got bad. Maybe when I get better I won't—"

Vickie watched her father shake his head as he cut in quickly. "No, Diane. Face up to the fact that you deliberately did something wrong, no matter how innocently it started. All through life we can always find someone or something to blame for our faults and mistakes."

He rubbed his forehead in a tired gesture, saying gently, "We are not pointing a finger of judgment at you, Diane. Vickie or Betty Lou might have done the same thing in your situation."

He stopped and reached for the Bible lying on one side of the desk. "I read in here that the heart is deceitful and desperately wicked, and I fully believe it. I see it so often in my profession. Everyone wants to go his own selfish way and do his own thing without regard for anyone else."

Mr. Montgomery's voice became unsure as he went on. "But these last months I have begun to discover that no one has to live in greedy unhappiness. There is a better way. The Bible says we can be made new through faith in Jesus Christ. We do not have to be ruled by how we feel or by our circumstances."

He gripped the Bible tightly. "You see, there is more to the Christmas story than just Christmas, just the birth of a baby. That is only the beginning of the story. It goes on beyond that to—to Easter. Not to new clothes and spring vacation and Easter bunnies, but to a cross, to death for the One who was born at Christmas. And even then, according to what I read in here, the story does not end there."

There was pleading in his eyes as he looked around at them. "I do not know how the story fits together. I am not even sure just why I am saying all this to you now."

Forgotten words from last summer's conversation with Pete flickered in Vickie's mind, and she said them out loud into the stillness of the room.

"Pete said someone told him a long time ago that anybody can ask God to forgive the wrong things they do. And if they are really sorry, He will."

Her father nodded agreement. "I gather Pete does not know much more about the Bible than I do, although we are both searching. He and I are like a couple of blind men trying to lead each other across an expressway."

His smile was faint and gone almost at once, swallowed by his earnestness to explain. He hurried on. "I do know just from my law experience that the only way to be forgiven—of anything—is to admit the wrong we've done."

"Admit—to God?"

Mr. Montgomery looked startled at Diane's question. "Yes—yes, I am sure you must admit it to God. Although, if He is God, He already knows it. But you must confess to the ones you have directly wronged."

"Betty Lou already knows," Diane said. Then, in a whisper, she asked, "Anna? *Must* I tell her?"

Mrs. Montgomery tightened her arm around Diane's shoulders. "Yes, Anna deserves your explanation. But you need not worry about it. You already know how understanding she is."

Diane's thin hands twisted together as she stared at the floor. "But—how can I tell my mother?" she pleaded.

Vickie stood up and walked over to Diane, reaching out her hand. "We'll go over together and tell your mother all about it as soon as she comes home from work."

The strength of her voice surprised even Vickie. Usually Diane was the one to take the lead and say, "Let's do this or that." But this time Diane needed advice and help. And

after all, what was a best friend for if not to be strong herself and to help her friend do the right thing even when it
was hard?